Praise for Keri Ford

"[A] fun, fast, and thoroughly enjoyable friends to lovers story."
—Slick Reads on *Through The Wall*

"Keri Ford has penned a marvelous short story of two characters that are totally right for each other and who should have given a relationship between them a try in the past."
—The Romance Studio on *On The Fence*

"I really appreciate Ms. Ford writing unique world realities into her plotlines. It helps to make her characters and their situations stand out amongst others in the same romance sub-genre."
—Top Pick! Night Owl Romance on *On The Fence*

"If you're looking for a quick read to get your heart sighing and your hormones racing, then I highly recommend *On the Fence*. It'll press all your happy buttons."
—Long and Short Romance Reviews on *On The Fence*

Cupcakes and Crushes

Keri Ford

Samhain Publishing, Ltd.
11821 Mason Montgomery Road, 4B
Cincinnati, OH 45249
www.samhainpublishing.com

Cupcakes and Crushes
Copyright © 2015 by Keri Ford
Print ISBN: 978-1-61922-931-0
Digital ISBN: 978-1-61922-679-1

Editing by Heidi Moore
Cover by Lyn Taylor

This book is a work of fiction. The names, characters, places, and incidents are products of the writer's imagination or have been used fictitiously and are not to be construed as real. Any resemblance to persons, living or dead, actual events, locale or organizations is entirely coincidental.

All Rights Are Reserved. No part of this book may be used or reproduced in any manner whatsoever without written permission, except in the case of brief quotations embodied in critical articles and reviews.

First Samhain Publishing, Ltd. electronic publication: April 2015
First Samhain Publishing, Ltd. print publication: April 2015

Acknowledgements

As always, a lot of effort goes into the making of a book. It takes a village and I appreciate all the people in mine.

Sasha Devlin, who always knows just what to say to push me through to get the book done.

My new critique partner, Julie Anne Lindsey. Your input was invaluable and I look forward to trading many more manuscripts with you.

My amazing new editor, Heidi Moore. She has a fabulous red pen… that probably needed new ink after me.

December Gephart, who was my number one hand-holder and partner in happy claps with the making of this book.

This book brought many new and wonderful things to my career, including my two extraordinary agents, Louise Fury and Victoria Lowes of the Bent Agency. I look forward to many more books with y'all!

My hometown served as a bit of inspiration in the writing of this book. It seems far-fetched to send a cupcake to every student at a school, but it's not. When a beloved member of our community fought a hard battle with cancer, my community continually rallied support. A student suggested everyone at the school receive a cupcake to celebrate if her scans came back better. The scans showed improvement and a local businessman commissioned a bakery to send every student at the school a cupcake for their support, hopes and prayers. #TeamCorrie.

Chapter One

Oh, dear heavens, Turtle Pine, Alabama. Home of the fierce Snapping Turtles. Their biggest claim to fame was consecutively winning the AA basketball state tournament for ten years straight.

Get. Me. Out. Of. Here.

The only reason Annie wasn't breathing in a paper bag while waiting for her suitcase to come around the baggage carousel, was because she knew she was only sticking around long enough to do a favor. Then it was back to the highly acclaimed bakery she worked at, where the booking for weddings was currently eighteen months in advance.

Step one of getting out of Turtle Pine the fastest was finding her ride to her grandparents' house. There was no tall, slender woman with an eye out for a hot date impatiently waiting for her. Not that Annie was shocked, but she had hoped for once her half-sister Tina would have something together besides her shirt matching her shoes.

Annie aimed her phone away from the sunlight pouring in through the glass front windows of Turtle Pine's regional airport. She scrolled through her contacts in a game of eeny, meeny, miny, moe in hopes of finding a ride from the airport to her grandparents. Her grandma didn't drive anymore, and Grandpa was uncomfortable going much farther than the grocery store with his broken wrist. Annie had two other half-sisters she could choose from, but she was only fine with calling one of them. Sadly, *that* sister didn't live in Turtle Pine. Out of four sisters, Mary was the only one who hadn't been raised by their grandparents.

Contact list it was. A total introvert who'd been gone from town for years? Annie sighed and scrolled some more. As if there wasn't enough fun packed into coming back home, it was surely about to get even more so. She shielded the screen with a magazine and attempted to tilt it a little more to choose from slim pickings when the shadow of a man moved over her.

"Annie?" The shadow belonged to a tall man who appeared to have shopped at Camouflage, Mud and More. His brow lifted a touch as his head tipped to the side. "Annie Cookie?"

That was her. Now who was he and—wow. She rubbed a hand under her nose to get a refreshing whiff of her hand lotion. He must be three days late for a shower. Once upon a time, you could have found her looking and smelling like that. She would have been making one of those goofy in-love grins through every last minute of it. The very thought of it flipped her stomach. She couldn't pin down if it was butterflies or nausea. They were simultaneously good and bad memories. "That's me."

His smile broadened. "You've changed since high school. I would give you a hug, but I'm so nasty." He extended a grimy hand her way.

There was something about his face that was vaguely, sort of familiar. By his greeting, she was one hundred percent sure she was supposed to recognize him. But her mind was all blank. Fake smile it was as she accepted his hand. Dear, God, please let her put a name to his face soon.

Dark mud filled under his nails and there was a stark, clean line on his wrist showing where he'd washed up. Had Turtle Pine's annual mud run been this morning? By the bags under his eyes, she didn't think he'd been doing that. The mud run was more fun and less exhausting. At least, that's how she remembered it. She hadn't actually participated in it since she was fourteen or so.

"Tina asked if I could pick you up."

Well, looked like Tina had come through after all. Sort of. Seeing as she hadn't seen her half-sister in years, it would have been nice to have the fairy tale where her sister greeted her with a hug and excited scream. Fairy tales hadn't existed for Annie in a long time though. She also doubted Tina had started caring about her in the time she'd been gone. "One of the kids have a ball game?"

They always had ball games. Baseball, football, soccer—hell, even a golf ball was included. She didn't have any confirmation, but based on Facebook, Tina's life ambition was to find a dad for her kids at an assortment of sporting events. Since one such candidate was standing in front of her, doing her bidding, she was succeeding.

He winced. "She'd probably wish it. She hasn't talked to you?"

What a laugh. "No. Grandma said she'd send Tina to pick me up. I sent her a text before my plane took off to remind her, but she never responded."

He didn't ask, but grabbed her suitcase and had it spun around and ready to roll all in one seamless move. "Her oldest and another kid from school snuck out last night, took her truck and got it stuck in a field. Took us hours to get it out and her boy got stung by some yellow jackets."

"Oh." Well, damn. Figures about the time she started thinking the worst, it would bite her on the ass to make her feel guilty. "Is he okay?"

"He's okay now. They were leaving the hospital about half an hour ago."

"That's good. I remember her mentioning he had some allergies." And good grief, when did Tina's son get old enough to drive? Sure,

Annie was out of the loop, but she could swear the boy was just twelve… thirteen?

"So that's why I'm here." He pointed at her, aiming his finger to her toes and back up the front of her. "Those washable?"

She looked down. "My clothes?"

"Yeah."

She rubbed a hand over the soft-pink, slinky material of her skirt. "Yes…why?"

He dusted the front of his shirt. Sunrays beaming through the windows showcased dust puffing off him. "Because we used my truck to get your sister's out of the mud."

"I see." And she still saw all the dust in the air. Her nose tickled and she rubbed at the tip in an attempt to resist a sneeze.

"I didn't have time to wash it." He started for the doors and the glass opened as he neared.

She glanced at the airport and considered a run for the ticket counter, but that would be useless. The next flight out of here wouldn't be for another week. It wasn't so bad yet that she was open to hitchhiking to Birmingham. Not to mention that somebody who she was supposed to know was walking away with most of her prized possessions in her suitcase. She stepped into the sunshine. Even though fall had landed and cooler air draped blessedly over grass dying off in the heat of summer, dampness coated her back. So different from the last time she'd stood here at the airport. With the thrill of escaping, the rush of going somewhere new, she couldn't recall if she'd been sweating or shivering. She had been leaving this place that had spit out so much misery they should rename it that. Misery, Alabama. Call the darn place for what it was.

There were only a handful of vehicles in the parking lot. All but one of them was clean. As for the one that wasn't...a thick knot landed in her throat. The last time she'd ridden in a truck that had more mud than paint on the side of it, she'd said bye-bye to her virginity. It had been blue and looked a lot like that dirty one in front of her. The topless Jeep with tires right up to her neck sat in the front corner lot. Clumps of dirt had plopped on the parking lot surrounding it. There were no running boards, so the undercarriage showed off the mud the tires had slung under there.

Oh boy. It was definitely butterflies dancing in her stomach, not nausea like she'd hoped for.

Shameful, really. Well, she *should* feel ashamed, but she wasn't as her knees were getting wobbly with each unsteady step toward the vehicle made for fun. A truck like that one had played a big part in why she'd gone to a city. Trucks like those always drove headfirst into bad decisions. She'd avoided bad decisions for years. Made a point to, as a matter of fact. Nothing about that was changing, no matter how appealing his truck looked.

It was time to get her keister to her grandparents' house before she put serious thought into ways to delay her trip. That bakery was the only reason she was back in this town. Specifically, she was back in town to fill in for her grandpa, and she would do well to remember that. He'd taught her everything about baking, decorating, and with some help from her grandma, all things about life in general. Of everything she'd been taught and learned and soaked up, she'd never once expected her grandma to utter the five words she had two days ago on the phone.

"Your grandpa needs your help."

As much as Annie hadn't wanted to return to Turtle Pine, she'd had her suitcase across her bed before she'd even found out why. Discovering

Grandpa had promised seven hundred cupcakes to the local school as well as a wedding cake had slowed her packing, but it hadn't stopped her.

Her driver, who would hopefully have his name written on something in his vehicle, because it was way too late now to admit she didn't have a clue who he was, grabbed the door handle. More dirt, and even some pine straw, raked off in his hand as he tugged it open and revealed a seat just as filthy. Hunks of mud and leaves and, God, she didn't even know what all was clumped on the seat. She could nearly feel the grit against her thighs, and it made her remember wind in her hair and cool muddy water being slung on her cheeks.

"I don't suppose you have any towels in your suitcase that you can sit on?" He rubbed his chin that carried a couple days' worth of good-looking facial hair. With his short-cut dark hair topping off tanned skin and statue-worthy muscles, calling him attractive was just scratching the surface. This guy couldn't have gone to her high school. A girl didn't forget a guy like him. Either that or he'd changed a shitton and she couldn't even begin to whittle his sex appeal off to fit someone from her fuzzy memory.

"I…" Lord, there she went. Blank. Her whole mind just blank. Hot truck and all of a sudden the man driving it went from that guy picking her up to hello, aren't you just an attractive drink of water?

She blinked and turned away to get the vehicle and the man out of sight. Trucks like this was why she'd started hanging out at the library halfway through high school. These kinds of vehicles didn't park at the public library. Also, since Tina had sent this guy, after he'd helped her with her kid, they were probably dating. That was a big heck-to-the-no and even more of a reason to get her head on straight. Here for work. Not for play.

Side trips into mud riding? That was off the table. "I'm sure I've got something."

She turned her bag around and opened it for the T-shirt she'd stuck down inside. The name of the bakery she worked at was printed across the front, but it was a size too big, stained with use and had been now downgraded to her sleep shirt. With all the food stains on it, why not add some mud too? Or she could just lift her skirt up a little and get that feeling of grit against her thighs.

Good grief, she needed something to drink to wet her dry throat. Ideas of hiking her skirt up to drive down the road wasn't exactly a ladylike thought like any her grandma had tried teaching her. She lifted the large plastic bag stuffed with her bakery tools and dug for the shirt.

"Did you pack a kitchen sink in there too?"

Her cheeks warmed over. He was looking? Her pulse kicked up a notch as her throat tightened. More than ever, she was in dire need of something to drink now. He was staring at her bag where her cotton granny panties were packed? She pushed her utensils over the top of the suitcase to hide the practical things. She hadn't come prepared for a man to pick her up from the airport in an attractive truck. If she'd known this was coming, she'd have rethought all her clothes—including the ones on her back. Cut-off shorts, flip-flops and a tank top sounded about right for something to change into. Pretty much all the things she'd left behind when she left this town.

Goodness, this was surely some kind of sickness. Even with the way he smelled vaguely of a swamp, if he offered to take her for a ride, she wasn't sure she could resist. It'd been too damn long since she'd seen a vehicle like this one and had the fun it promised to deliver. She needed to resist any kind of man who drove one. Back woods. Muddy roads. She'd been gone for years, but she hadn't forgotten about that pond tucked in along those old trails.

So maybe there were some parts of Turtle Pine, Alabama that weren't too bad.

She cleared her throat and stuffed her hair back. "Grandpa asked me to come in and help with the shop. I brought a few of the tools I like."

"Looks like enough for a whole kitchen in there."

"Just about." She pasted on a friendly smile. She couldn't go the rest of the day not knowing who this guy was. Maybe if she put a name to the face, recalled he'd been a dick to her in school, then she could focus all her energy where it should be—on her grandparents. "I didn't catch your last name."

"Revlin." He chuckled, and that sound did tingly things to the hairs on her neck. His grin wasn't so bad either as he hooked his thumbs in his belt loops. But the name, oh heavens, the name was all kinds of wrong. "It's me, Annie. Cade Revlin. I thought you knew who I was."

She paused in her search through her bag and looked up. Another knot touched the back of her throat. "Revlin. Like Sheriff James Revlin?" She cleared her throat. Younger brother to… No, she wouldn't say that. Best to stick to his dad. "That is, if he's still the sheriff."

He nodded and smiled. "That's my dad and, yep, he's still holding down the fort at the department."

She looked him over, trying to fit this man's frame into the kid she remembered. "Oh my God. Cade. Little Rev."

He chuckled. "Nobody's called me that since school."

The last time she'd seen him was then. "I'm sorry. I didn't even recognize you."

Obviously. Wait. If that was Little Rev then was that…

Oh my God.

She took another look at the Jeep—a closer look. Under the brown clumps along the side was red paint. Air seeped from her chest and the tight knot in her throat eased. Red, not blue. Not the same truck. Thank heavens for little blessings. That would have been too awkward for words, and believe it or not, probably the only thing to put her libido on ice.

Little Rev had grown up and looked nothing like his older brother. From the height, the build, the scruff on his chin and dark hair. She took time for another look, trying to find some similarity with the older brother she had known a little too well. She found nothing.

Except for their taste in vehicles. They had that in common to a T.

Cade patted his stomach. "Mom made me start eating all my potatoes and rolls. She was determined to put weight on me before the wind carried me off."

"Well—" she tucked hair behind her ear, "—it worked."

She wished mashed potatoes and rolls would do to her body what it had done to his. His tight jeans and tucked-in shirt said there was a flat belly under there. His arms stretched the snug cotton. His shoulders were broad enough he shaded her from the sun. Heat curled through her body. Was it suddenly warmer outside?

She got her hands around the shirt in her suitcase and tugged it out. "Your, ah, Mrs. Revlin should market that diet plan."

"I think she does. She calls it Sunday lunch and anyone is welcome to attend."

She chuckled and put her suitcase back in order as he took her shirt and turned for the truck. He pounded the seat, loosening the dried mud. Little hard balls of dirt bounced and he swept most of it off to the floorboard. He spread her shirt over the seat and he faced her while swiping his hands.

He paused and frowned toward her feet. "Are you going to be able to get in wearing those shoes?"

Definitely. She tried to keep her smile more polite and less eager beaver. "I can manage."

She grabbed her skirt, hiked it halfway up her thighs and set her foot. The oh-shit handle was right where it needed to be. With a satisfying tug, she pulled herself up and was in the seat. Like a glove.

"Nicely done." He pushed the door closed.

"Thank you."

"Some girls can't manage it in tennis shoes. I have to pick them up."

Well, if I'd have known that was an option… Bad Annie! This was why she'd quit cold turkey all those years ago. Being five days late for a monthly confirmation from her uterus had scared her butt out of trucks like this one and right into hard wooden chairs at the library. Where there were librarians who watched and chatted with her and in general made it impossible to be doing things with boys that she shouldn't be doing. Those cold chairs and being surrounded by the steady thump of the librarian checking books in and out had saved her hide. She'd not only left tempting trucks driven by grinning, shirtless boys behind, she'd gotten clean out of town and traded them for a promising future.

He put her suitcase in the back and then climbed in behind the wheel. He cranked the engine with a heavy foot over the gas that caused a good rumbling.

The vibrations hummed through the seat, flaking a few crumbs of dirt down the back of her shirt. That's how a truck was supposed to sound and move. She ran her thumbs over the seams of the armrest of the door. It was made for back roads, mud and squeezing between trees.

Sweat against the seat and sun on your cheeks. Every last bit of it made better by a hot guy behind the steering wheel with an ice chest between them. Especially if the guy stripped his shirt off.

He put the truck in drive and pulled away from the airport. "I guess I'm taking you to your grandma's?"

She nodded. "Yeah. I don't know where I'm going after that, but she said I could use her car."

"Good. It's real awesome what you're doing."

A sense of pride overwhelmed her for a bit. "I'd do anything for them. They were there for me. It wouldn't be right to not be here."

"I know all the kids are happy."

Work. Work was a good, focused thing to talk about, and she wasn't letting this conversation end until the old wood of her grandma's porch was creaking under her heels. "Why did he promise all those cupcakes?"

"Motivation. The football field needed a makeover. He said if they got out there, worked hard and had it all looking like it was supposed to before the season started, he'd bake them all a cupcake each. They got it done."

"Sounds like Grandpa."

"But I don't just mean being there for your grandpa. You're also taking over the wedding."

She lifted her shoulder. "Might as well while I'm here. Brides plan so far out in advance. It's not like you can just blindly pick a bakery out of the phone book a week before your wedding."

He looked a little surprised at that with the way he shot her a quick glance with raised eyebrows. "No cake probably would have ruined the wedding."

"It certainly would have messed up the pictures at the reception."

She lifted a shoulder. "There's nothing else like wedding cake. I swear, I use the same ingredients with a wedding cake as a birthday cake, and still…there's this extra taste with the wedding cake."

"You're starting to sound like a romantic."

"I haven't made a cake yet that I wouldn't enjoy a good romance with." Not to mention cake had this dependable aspect. She leaned against the truck, settling in more and finding herself comfortable in town when not half an hour ago, she'd been dreading every step. Work wasn't just some focus. It was good. It was her purpose. "You don't think wedding cake is special?"

"Cake is cake, I guess."

"Bah." She readjusted, tucking a foot under her and facing him a little more while the wind kept her hair flying out of her face. "It's not only the cake that's different. Everything is. The size, the decorations, the uniqueness applied to each cake. Sure, birthday cakes are special, and some can really wow you, but *every* wedding cake wows you."

"I guess."

"Just the sheer time it takes to make a cake is different. I've spent days working on nothing but one wedding cake. That's it. One wedding cake. By the time I'm done and it's put together, my back aches from being bent over, my fingers are cramped from holding the pastry bag and there's so much grit in my eyes, they're practically living off eye drops." She breathed. "But when you're finished, there's this indescribable awe. And then I get that awe again when the bride comes in and sees the cake for the first time."

"I hope you're right and it'll still be worth it. I don't know much about the wedding details. I know my niece is dressed like a fairy flower girl instead of a princess, but from what I've picked up, your sister has a doozy planned."

Annie frowned. "My sister?"

He nodded. "Jane."

Why in the world would Jane have any input on the cake? Why would Cade's niece be… Unless…no.

No.

A nervous chuckle went over her. She wasn't exactly on speaking terms with Jane, but somebody would have told her that her sister was getting married. By not exactly, she meant, not at all. Still. Marriage. That gossip was sure to float down a chain somewhere. Facebook at least. Or by someone like, oh, she didn't know, her grandma for starters when she'd called last week.

There was that feeling again. That dread sitting heavy and hard in the pit of her stomach. The one that had been there since she'd left home and gotten on the airplane. One that about had her wanting to make a dash back to the ticket counter to take a flight to anywhere but here. "I hope you're about to tell me Jane quit her job and became a wedding planner."

Cade slid his gaze to hers and then back to the road. He turned at the corner, putting them on her grandparents' street. "You don't know?"

She pointed at her face. "Does this look like the face of someone who knows something?"

"Not so much." He rubbed the back of his head and dropped his arm with a breath. "Damn it, I thought you knew. Jane's the one getting married. To Peter."

Holy mother, Annie was going to be sick. That heavy pit of despair in her belly exploded. She was about two seconds away from full-on blowing-chunks sick. Her cheeks cooled, but her head filled with warmth.

19

She put a hand over her stomach as houses and trees flew past.

The wind from the open-top Jeep should have made her feel better. That was the rule of riding in a car, wasn't it? Get sick, open a window. My goodness, she could hang her head out the side like a dog right now and wouldn't find relief.

"Hold on. Almost there." Cade's voice was a soothing little sliver of a chill pill going through her mind.

Just not enough. "I think I'm going to be sick."

"It ain't going to hurt this truck any. Don't get it on me and we'll be fine."

She laughed. A little more ease settled through her tumbling stomach. She sat back against the seat. Dirt embedded in the fibers of the cushioned seat rubbed comfortably with the cold sweat on the back of her neck. A good little gritty distraction. He turned into her grandma's drive and stopped the truck.

It didn't stop all of her churning, but it was down to manageable levels.

He twisted and rested an arm over the steering wheel. "I'm sorry. I thought you knew. I wouldn't have said anything."

She reached over and patted his hand. "It's okay. I'd rather find out now than later when she walks in and says, 'Hey, you're making this for me'. Grandma knew I wouldn't have agreed if she'd have told me who it was for."

"Just think of all the kids you're going to make happy now that you're here."

"Oh, I would have come for them. I would have left after I delivered the last cupcake." It was petty and sounded terrible, but she really didn't care. Getting to turn her back on her sister—even after all these years—

felt like the sweet justice she'd been waiting to deliver. And in the form of refusing to make a cake—a sweet? Oh man, she was practically foaming here at the idea of it. She glanced over and tried to look sorry about it, but she wasn't feeling it. "I know this is your brother's wedding and you probably think I'm horrible for even saying that out loud."

He lifted his shoulder. "All I know is you and Peter were together, and then he was making out with Jane."

Yeah, that was a good roundup of the story. There were a lot of middle parts in there. Hugs and concerns from her sister. A couple of, *"Don't worry, Annie. I'll talk to him."* Just when Annie had thought she was going to get the supportive sister who'd have her back like she'd always wanted, Jane stuck her tongue in Peter's mouth and put her hands in places they shouldn't have been.

After all these years, finally, this was her moment to stick it to them. She was pretty sure she was supposed to be too old for those kinds of thoughts. Then again, revenge was best served cold, they say. "Last I was here, the grocery store sold box mix and canned frosting. They can do that together."

He chuckled and got out of the truck. "Let me get your bag."

She sat forward in the vehicle and stared down. Getting married. Last she knew, they'd broken up. Then gotten back together. Back apart. She knew this because that's usually when people who didn't talk to her attempted to. To see if she was getting back with Peter now that he wasn't with Jane. That had been her life for two long, miserable years until Annie had gotten out of town, left that fun dance behind and hadn't kept up since. At times, it seemed like a lifetime ago. Today? Felt more like yesterday.

Cade opened her door and leaned on the frame. It brought him in closer and nearly towering over her.

She glanced to him. "I don't want him back. I never did."

He lifted a shoulder. "I'm not judging you."

She sat back in the seat, rubbed the top of her thighs and straightened her dress. "I don't want you to think I want him back or anything. Not wanting to do their wedding cake isn't jealousy. I just plain and simply don't want any part of their lives mixing in mine."

"Watching them cut a homemade cake sitting on a foil board could be fun."

She laughed. "I would actually love to see that."

"Guess you won't be going to the wedding?"

"I wasn't even invited."

"I'll take pictures for you."

She swung her legs out and faced him. "You know why I don't want to do the cake at the wedding. This is your brother getting married. How come you're on my bandwagon?"

He leaned in a little closer. "Is it fine if I'm completely honest?"

"Sure."

"I always liked you better than your sister."

She blinked and had no words. Not what she'd been thinking. At all. So. Not. Thinking…that.

He lifted a shoulder. "I'm sorry he did it, but I'm also a little glad my brother cheated on you. If he hadn't, y'all might have gotten married, and the rest of my life would be one awkward, uncomfortable moment after another."

Oh, boy. Holy hell, Little Rev was not little anymore, and he was coming on to her like no man ever had. Boy, oh, boy. Except. She eyed him. "You're dating my other sister, Tina, aren't you?"

He straightened like she'd hit him. "No. Where did you hear that?"

"She asked you to pick me up. You helped her last night. I thought—"

He put his hand up, stopping her. "I'm a deputy. That's why I helped her last night. She asked me to get you from the airport because I was standing there when your grandma called to remind her."

He got her about the waist, lifted and stood her on her feet on the ground. At least, she thought they were her feet. "I…uh." She cleared her throat. "Okay. I don't know what to say."

"Then don't say anything."

Chapter Two

Cade rubbed damp palms over his stiff jeans one more time as he drove away from Annie. He'd walked her to the porch, set her bag on the steps next to her and waved bye.

She'd done little more than smile and softly chuckle, but oh man, that *smile*. Not just any polite smile like she'd given him at the airport. This had been something else altogether. Her cheeks had colored and her hazel eyes brightened with flecks of green in them sparkling like emeralds.

He couldn't believe he'd just talked to Annie that way. In his bedroom mirror when he was fifteen, he'd talked to her like that all the time. Now she was here, but he still shouldn't be saying those things, not even when she smiled at him like that.

He was sure nothing would turn her smile upside-down faster than bringing up her sisters. She'd just about thrown up in his truck the last time. Even though admitting that two of her sisters, Tina and Jane, were making his life a living hell could potentially bring them some common ground, he didn't want to risk it.

He pulled into a bay at the car wash. In case another moment came up that he could take Annie somewhere, he would have his truck spotless so there wouldn't be any excuses. He couldn't risk her riding with someone else because they might have a cleaner vehicle.

It had almost killed him to pick her up with his truck looking like it did, but he hadn't had a choice. To stop and wash it would have made him late to get her—risking that she'd have called someone else. Risking being late hadn't been an option.

Jim was going to kill him for the mud mess he was about to make in the wash rack, but it couldn't be helped. He cashed in a ten for quarters and got to work. No sooner did the water get started, his brother pulled up behind him.

"Damn." Peter pushed his door closed with a hard slam. "He must have buried Tina's truck."

"Pretty much." Cade started at the top over the rack bars and opened his door to let the water pour out. "Big thanks for coming to help and all. It was your future sister-in-law and nephew."

"Ah—" Peter chuckled, "—I knew you could handle it, and then you got the reward from Tina."

Not only Tina and Jane on his ass, but Peter too. One stupid get-a-man-for-a-day auction that his mom had dreamed up to raise money for the animal shelter, and suddenly his life was a train wreck. Tina had put in the high bid for him and hadn't let him go. Next time the shelter was low on food, he'd take out a loan and support the shelter himself. "The only reward I got was running her son to the hospital and being stuck there for about six hours."

Of course, all that had led to the fantastic reward of nabbing Annie from the airport, but he'd leave that part out. Annie-Lyn as he'd so often thought of her. Annie-Lyn was mysterious and refined. An untouchable, expensive item in a museum that had always been out of his reach.

Peter rested against the front of the wash stall. "When the stress and worry of her son eases, Tina will remember that you helped her out."

"It'd be great if she wouldn't." A futile wish. A genie in a lamp couldn't make that happen.

Peter frowned. "I thought y'all were dating?"

"Fuck no." For about the hundredth time in the last six or so months. Fuck. No. Not now, not ever. Cade glanced over and then focused back on his washing. "I've told you that. Why do you keep thinking we are?"

"That's what Jane said. I heard her telling one of her friends last week."

God. He'd squashed this rumor last month. A rumor started by Jane in the past. Tina another time. It was official. He wasn't telling anybody that Annie was in town or that she wasn't planning to make their cake for the wedding of the year. In fact, he'd like to somehow help her not make that cake, if that was possible. Ideas came to him of ways he could keep Annie so distracted that she'd never even reach the bakery. "We're not dating. And we're not going to. Please make that clear to Jane so she'll quit saying it."

"It's not all made up. She said y'all are going out. You took Tina to dinner."

No. That was not at all how that had happened. He'd gone to Jaspers *alone*. Tina had showed up after he'd ordered and the place was packed. Tina had asked to sit with him. He'd been being neighborly and said sure. What else was he supposed to do? Pack up his half-eaten food and leave? Tell her no in front of the whole town? Rock. Hard place. Him. That had been his life since the auction. At restaurants. Gas stations. The grocery store. It was like the woman had broken into his house and stuck a GPS tracker under his skin in his sleep.

The closer they got to the wedding, the more often he saw her. Jane, for some reason, didn't seem to come to Mom's house anymore without Tina attached to her hip. "Jane's confused."

Peter frowned. "It's part of why we ordered the bridesmaids and groomsmen like we did. So you and Tina could be partners."

Great. He hadn't heard this yet. "Thanks, but, no thanks."

"It also means you get to sit with each other at the rehearsal dinner and the reception."

The reception that was going to be lacking the main centerpiece. He grinned. Getting to see the look on Jane's face after the problems she kept causing him with this whole Tina mess made it even more worth it to hold back the information. "Don't do things the hard way on my behalf. Partner whoever you want, however you want."

"All right. I'll tell her."

Good luck getting her to listen. "Thanks."

"I don't know why you're so against Tina. She's beautiful."

On the outside, he could agree. On the inside, she was this creature from another dimension he didn't want any part of it. The stalking was getting more than a little creepy. The fact that she was his neighbor didn't help. He'd started closing his blinds long ago.

"What are you doing today?"

"I'm thinking about going to bed as soon as I finish this."

Peter checked his phone and frowned. "It's ten in the morning."

"And I've been awake since six yesterday morning." He moved along the side of the truck and got under the fender. "Did you need help with something?"

"Nah. I'm heading out to the pond for fishing and didn't know if you wanted to go."

Sounded like the perfect opportunity to be cornered by his future sister-in-law and surprised by Tina with a picnic basket. Yes, his life had come to that. And yes, he knew perfectly well Tina's son had just gotten out of the hospital, Cade still wouldn't put it past her. She was that aggressive. Or maybe desperate. He didn't know. He didn't want to get close enough to find out. Eventually, her interest would fade. It had with every other one of his friends she'd randomly set her sights on. Cade seemed to be pushing the limits of her usual interest since they were up to half a year. Best he recalled she'd given up after four or so months with his friends. Cade had to be getting near the finish line with her.

His brother waited for an answer, so he shook his head. "I'm really tired and I'll just fall asleep on y'all."

"I'll holler at you tomorrow then."

"Okay." Though Cade didn't know what for and he wasn't sure he wanted to find out. He swept around the front of his truck and pulled his winch out to clean the cable. This was going to cost him at least another ten dollars.

Fifteen dollars and forty-five minutes later, Cade pulled from the wash and headed to the house. He had about three things on his mind. A hot shower, a bite to eat and Annie-Lyn. Not necessarily in that order.

Rarely in that order and sometimes, all three of those things at once. He readjusted in his seat and turned on his block. It took about two seconds to spot the white truck in the driveway next to his and even less time for a curse to roll off his tongue.

It was starting to be a habit. See that truck, start cussing. He needed to move. Seriously, move and fast. He slowed and pulled in his driveway. Maybe what he needed was a garage. With an automatic door on it instead of just this open carport. He could slip in and out with privacy.

It wasn't that he truly thought Tina stared out her kitchen window and waited for him to get home, but people living two blocks over heard him pull up in his truck. The noise was hard to miss. He could park his truck and drive his cop car all the time, but it was almost winter. Soon it would be too cold for the open-top Jeep. Already it was getting close to that anyway, and then he'd be forced to park it. He pulled his keys, hopped out and ran to the door. He got his key in the knob and—

"Cade!" Her voice called out. It used to be a somewhat pleasant sound. It could have even been classified as a friendly sound. Now it had this pitch with this annoying thing in there that he couldn't quite get his finger on. "Wait up!"

He sighed and got his door unlocked so he could make a break inside as fast as he could. She hurried around the corner, running on her tip toes like she was dodging giant piles of dog shit. A dog…maybe that's what he needed. The biggest dog he could find to leave big piles of shit all over his yard to keep this woman away. Being frank with Tina would likely end in a number of unwanted scenarios, largely including a shriek from his mom that could be heard across the county. He'd tried polite nos and avoidance. Tina wasn't getting the message. And she had this manipulative way about her, that if he got any bolder, she'd somehow make him out to be the bad guy.

He needed another woman. Annie-Lyn came to mind, but she was only here temporarily. Turtle Pine didn't offer much when it came to females. They all seemed to be married or too young. Either literally too young that he wasn't going there or way too young at heart, which was far worse. That left single moms. He liked kids, so that wasn't a turn off. It was just, other than Tina, they were all busy being single moms to their young kids. They tended not to make time for anything else. "How's Pat doing?"

"Good. All the swelling and redness is gone. I wanted to thank you for the help last night. I don't know what I would have done if you hadn't been here."

If he were to guess, she'd have flipped through PTA contacts for single dads. "I'm just glad he's okay."

She gestured over her shoulder with her thumb. "I made some brunch if you're hungry."

Brunch, what was that anyway? Make some damn pancakes and call it a late breakfast. Or sandwiches and there you go…an early lunch. It didn't matter if he'd lived on vending machines for the last twenty-four hours—and he had—*brunch* at her house still wasn't happening. "Thanks for the offer, but I'm good."

"Oh." She dropped back in her heels. "If you change your mind, I have plenty."

"I'll let you know." He turned for the door.

"I was going to help wash your truck. Or well, do it for you. Least I could do."

So close, but no escape. "Thanks, but I've already got it taken care of."

She lifted a shoulder. "Maybe next time."

He just smiled and nodded to avoid continuing conversation and turned for the privacy of his house. He made it as far as getting the knob twisted.

"Oh, Jane called me about the wedding."

Damn. No cigar. "Did something change?"

"She said you could pick up your tux Wednesday."

Right. Like he'd already been told. "Good to know."

"And for the rehearsal dinner, she said it wasn't anything super fancy, but she didn't want anyone to wear jeans, so church nice is fine."

"Her wedding. She gets to make the choices."

Tina laughed, but it wasn't like Annie's laugh. There was so much emptiness in it. A hallow, fake noise. Pounding on an overturned paint bucket instead of a set of drums. "So anyway, I'm going into town tomorrow to pick up a new dress. Would you like me to grab you a new shirt or something while I'm there?"

God, this woman was so weird. They weren't dating. They didn't go out. They only talked when she managed it. Sure, this was a small town, but buying him clothes? Line crossed. This was the hard part about telling her he wasn't interested. She didn't come on to him directly. It was insertions in his life that most people would probably think was just being friendly. But she hadn't been this friendly last April before that stupid auction. "Thanks, but I've got something. If there's nothing else, I've got to get."

"Oh, are you going out tonight?"

He considered his words carefully. He'd seen this tactic in action before and watched a buddy of his take her to the movies. He also knew her better than to say he was resting all day or she might be knocking later with supper. "Just over to Mom's."

She smiled and her head tipped to the side. "Oh, I adore your mom. I haven't seen her in a week or more. Such a sweet, sweet lady to talk to."

Yes, his mom was. She was also ringleader number one who'd painted a Turtle Pine most-wanted-bachelor target on his back. The one and only upside to Tina personally trying to stab that bull's-eye was random girls were no longer appearing around Mom's table for Sunday lunch. "She'll be at the wedding Sunday, so I bet you'll catch her then."

"Oh. Well, I guess you're right." She laughed and he wasn't sure why.

"All right, I'll see you later." He got the door open and managed a foot inside and everything.

"Bye, and thanks again."

Instead of risking any words, he waved and closed himself in.

That woman was exhausting. He leaned back against his door. He had to move. Had to move soon. Or maybe the woman could wake up and take a hint one day. With how aggressive she was with polite refusals, he was terrified of what sort of beast she'd turn into with a firm no and being told to go away.

His truck might get turned into a prop for a man-hating country song.

He dragged his feet for a quick shower and to get back out. 'Cause sure enough, as soon as he fell asleep on the couch, she'd be knocking on the door saying she'd noticed he was still there and knew he was supposed to meet his mom.

Chapter Three

Annie stood on her grandma's porch until the hum of Cade's engine was long gone. A few fall leaves rolled across the ground and crinkled in the wind. Otherwise, it was quiet on the street. So quiet she could still clearly hear Cade's words echoing through her head in his deep timbre. With no distractions, the memory of him was powerful. He remained a comfortable feeling that hugged her skin and left her warm. To be honest, she didn't want to quite let it go. She pushed hair away from her face, trying to figure out what that had all been about and unable to put her finger on any of it.

Cade. Little Rev. She had visions of a somewhat scrawny guy. He would have been sixteen when she'd graduated and left. Only fourteen when she'd dated his older brother. She tried matching the quiet guy in the back of her head to this new version, but after seeing him today, that boy in her mind was such a distant memory she couldn't find him at all.

After she'd broken up with Peter and made an effort to stay away from him, she hadn't been in the same places as Cade. She'd done her best to avoid all the Revlins, as a matter of fact. If she wasn't at home, that had meant she was likely at the library, because like hell was Peter hanging out there.

He'd been too busy being popular and seeing girls. Girls like her sister.

"Ugh." She grabbed her bag and stepped in her old house.

Reminiscing was exactly why she'd never wanted to come back to this town. When she'd left, she'd left all of it in the past. Now bam. She'd been here not even an hour and all this crappy stuff was flying at her face.

Scents of sugar and baking and all the familiar smells that set a smile on her face and a rumbling in her stomach lifted the conflicting feelings off her as she stepped inside the old brick home. The standard old plate loaded down with cookies was in the center of the table like always. She couldn't remember a single day where she walked in and there wasn't something on that plate.

"Grandma?" she called. "Grandpa?" The old couch squeaked. Annie would know that sound anywhere.

Her grandma stepped around the corner looking much as Annie remembered. White hair pulled up. Cheeks red and full of purpose as she walked. "Annie!"

Annie stepped into the hug she had been missing. "Hey, Grandma."

"I've missed that face." She patted her on the cheek. "You shouldn't stay gone so long."

"I know." She didn't have anything to say beyond that. "How is Grandpa feeling?"

She patted Annie's back. "He's doing okay. Arm doesn't hurt anymore, just frustrating to live with. He's down at Mark's shop drinking coffee and probably lost track of the time. Getting old. He can't remember nothing anymore. Especially things like when one of his granddaughters is coming into town. I know it's hard for you to get away, and at the last minute, so thanks for stepping in to help him."

Annie put her stuff down and pulled out a seat at the table. "It's okay. He needed me, so here I am."

"Good. I wish you were here for just a visit so you wouldn't have to spend your whole time working."

Well, no worries there since after the cupcakes, Annie was D-O-N-E—done. "Is there anything special I need to know about the cupcakes?"

Her grandma shook her head. "Not that I've heard. Your grandpa hasn't given me a lot of details, just that about half need to be white and half chocolate. He mentioned you'd have to make a food order. Write down what you need and he'll get you the number to call it in. You can get a truck Tuesday or Thursday, I believe."

"When's the due date for these?"

"The school and all the kids are planning to see them Friday on the day of the first pep rally. He would have called you sooner, but he really thought he could do it with my help. We tried a couple practice runs, but it didn't work. He could have changed the delivery date, but everyone is looking forward to them before the first game, and he didn't want to disappoint everybody."

"It's fine. Don't even worry about me taking off work or anything like that. I'm glad I get to be here. If supplies come it will be no problem to have them by Friday."

"He left all the notes for the wedding cake at the bakery too. He said they were on his desk. He was afraid I'd throw them away when I was cleaning if they came home."

Annie's jaw clenched and she barely resisted grinding her teeth together. Too bad Grandpa hadn't brought them home. "I'm not sure I'll need them."

Her grandma's brows lifted. "You don't think so?"

"No, because I'm not doing Jane and Peter's wedding cake."

Her grandma visibly sank. "Annie."

She lifted her shoulder. "Were y'all even going to tell me that's who the cake was for?"

"I planned to tell you over the phone."

"I noticed you didn't."

She stared toward the center of the table. "I know. I'm sorry. I didn't know how to work it in."

A short sentence would have sufficed. "I'll do the cupcakes. I would have come just for the cupcakes. I'm done after them. Jane will have to find someone else. Or make it herself." Cade filled her head and she resisted the smile trying to take her face. He was right. Watching them cut an uneven rectangle over a foil-wrapped platter would be delightful.

"Annie, your sister needs you."

Funny. Annie remembered a time when she was scared. Not just scared—abso-freaking-lootly-terrified. By chance, Jane had found Annie crying. Since Annie had been wallering at the bottom of what she'd thought was rock bottom, she had dumped it all out. Her period was late. She was pregnant and fifteen. *"I'll talk to him and see,"* Jane had said. For those few precious moments, Annie had actually thought she was getting the sister she'd always wanted. Yeah. Hard for Jane to talk with Peter when parts of him were in her mouth. No fairy-tale sister bond, no Prince Charming either. Just a scary as hell wake-up call.

Annie blinked and wished she could forget the hurt those memories brought on. "I'm still not doing her wedding."

"Don't do it for her. Do it for me and your grandpa."

"Doing it for you two would still be doing it for her. And I'm not spending days on end making something for her."

Grandma narrowed her eyes into razor-sharp slits that used to terrify

Annie. "There is no one else. You know that. You know what scheduling is like. The wedding is Sunday. She can't find a good replacement that fast."

As fierce as Grandma's tone was, it wasn't enough. "It's Monday. She can get one from Wal-Mart before the weekend. Or make one."

"Annie." Her grandma leveled her with a look and settled her palms flat on the table. "Seeing each of you girls with your dream cake has been something your grandpa has talked about for years. Now one of you finally gets married and he breaks his wrist." She shook her head. "But you...you could do something even better than he could ever imagine for her."

Annie sat back. "I never said I couldn't do something amazing."

Hell, last month she'd made a giant Longhorn for the college to kick off football season. A bull. Out of cake. Complete with sprawling horns and smoke coming from his nostrils. She could make any damn thing she wanted. That was the key though. She could make anything *she wanted*.

"Then do it for her."

"I don't want to." She could make a donkey's ass. That she would do. Let the donkey bend down on his front knees and have his tail kicked up with a big toothy grin. Perfect.

Grandma reached across the table and patted her hand. "I know you and Jane have your differences. Be the bigger person."

Clearly, Grandma didn't know the whole story. Since telling it would involve going into Annie's teenage sex life, she would pass. "I don't want to be the bigger person. I want to be tiny. And petty. And go back home with that in my black heart."

Grandma's brows lowered. "Annie-Lyn, that is enough."

"You can't force me. I don't live here. I have my own life. I'm sorry.

I know you wanted something different, but I just can't." Her throat was tight. "I can't," she repeated for herself more than for her grandma. "I left here with the intent of leaving those two behind. I've done that, and I'm not getting dragged back."

"You know, it wasn't easy for her to accept you making her cake in your grandpa's place."

"I'm sure it was real hard for her to consider using me for something." Goodness, she all but forced her eyes not to roll. If only for the fact that Grandma would whack them back straight before they even finished making the round trip. "It sounds like she considered other options. She should explore those."

"Her only other option was to move the wedding date."

"Then problem solved."

Grandma pushed up from the table and went to the refrigerator. "Who knows how long that will be? And the invitations have already been sent. The church booked. The florist. You know those things can't just be pushed back on a whim—not even in a small town like ours. She didn't think you'd do it either."

"She was right."

"So prove her wrong."

Annie pushed up from the table with a small laugh. "I'm not a teenager anymore, Grandma. You can't push me into things by daring me."

"It was worth a shot." She opened a Sprite. "What would it take to get you to do the cake? You want an apology from her? I think at this point, you could get whatever you wanted from Jane."

"I don't want anything from her. I don't even want to see her." She turned around and stared out the window. Fall was closing in, but the trees were still thriving with green leaves. The lawn was neatly cut. Sunday afternoon was glaring down, and even through the pane of glass, laughter could be heard from kids playing down the street. A street she'd once played on. When she was young, she'd foolishly thought she'd have kids one day playing in this very same yard.

Then everything happened and it all changed. Nothing could ever bring back those old dreams. Annie had vowed to leave and that had been her focus.

Annie had plain and simply cut her half-sisters out of her life and had no desire to glue them back in. Tina had never even wanted to be friends. After hooking up with Peter, Jane hadn't tried pushing her way back in, so as far as Annie was concerned, not speaking to each other was mutual. "You say the invitations have been sent. Guess who didn't get one? I didn't even know she was getting married until Cade told me on the way here."

"Cade?"

Ugh. All that. She flipped her wrist. "Tina's oldest was stung by some yellow jackets. She asked Cade to pick me up from the airport."

Grandma's brows dipped in worry. "Oh, I haven't heard from her. I guess everything is okay?"

She wasn't surprised Grandma had no idea her oldest great-grandson had spent half the night in the hospital. Tina was the one who flitted around and tended to put herself first. Jane was everyone's favorite snake in the grass. Mary, their youngest sister, was the smart one, best Annie knew of her. Of all of them, Mary was the only one who'd lived with their dad. They'd only seen her for a little bit in the summer. Then there was Annie. The forgettable one. "Everything is fine, according to Cade."

She glanced down and caught sight of the family photos Grandma kept on the window sill. One with Tina and Jane taken when they'd still lived with Dad and their mom. The photo had been snapped maybe a year before their mom had died. The year before they'd moved to Turtle Pine to also be raised by Grandma and Grandpa alongside Annie. Annie had only been three, but she could remember being sat down at that kitchen table. A big plate of cookies had been in front of her and she'd munched her way through them as Grandma and Grandpa had talked about her new sisters coming to live with her. How they might be sad for a while, but they knew Annie would show the girls the ropes and be a great sister.

Another frame held a snapshot of Mary with Dad and her mom. All three of them were nothing more than strangers to Annie. She'd seen Mary a few weeks here and there over the years. Not often. Dad—she shook her head—had she ever seen him for more than one day? Not that she remembered. It had been more like hours at a time. Two was probably pushing it.

Another photo was of Annie with her grandparents. She touched over the top of her picture. She was lucky her dad's parents had found out about her and gotten her before her mom had left her for child services. God only knew where she would have ended up.

Three seemingly separate families. Four sisters varying from half-siblings to full thanks to Dad's wandering. What a mess.

Grandma was silent, and Annie glanced over her shoulder to find her sitting at the table with a cookie in her hand. Annie walked back, picked one from the pile and sat down again too.

Her grandma broke her cookie in half. "You know, you seem disappointed that you didn't get an invitation."

"I'm not. I guess I'm a little taken back that I didn't even know she was engaged, let alone getting married, then I come home and she expects me to build her wedding cake for her wedding that's Sunday." Hell, even the snobbiest of snobs who walked in the bakery in Texas knew what sort of payout that was. As in the four and five figure pay-off-your-car-loan-and-book-a-week-vacation-on-a-private-beach kind of payout. Sometimes more, depending on the size of the cake. Jane wanted her to just drop everything and do it for her? Annie didn't downshift that fast. She could see her grandparents coming up with this idea. She was more than happy to fill in for her grandpa, to make whatever cake he'd promised to whatever random stranger, but for Jane to go along with it? Um, no.

"Well, Annie, I don't know what to tell you. You don't participate or stay in contact with the family. You can't exactly get your panties in a twist when you don't know something."

That was the excuse now. What was it when she'd lived here before? She blended into the background. On purpose. After she broken up with Peter, she'd wanted to disappear. And unless Jane and Peter were breaking up, everyone let her. Nobody asked what was wrong. Nobody had cared that a once outgoing girl who'd lived for sports and fun was suddenly the biggest book hog this side of the Mississippi. Everyone had let her disappear. So far as she understood, nobody had noticed she was gone either. "I know."

She put the cookie down and rubbed her face. It wasn't even that she'd wanted the damn invitation. It wasn't like she would have come. She dropped her hands to her lap. "I guess I'm just surprised Jane has the gall to want me to do her cake. That's all. If it was the other way around, there's no way I would show my face to ask for something. And she didn't even have the guts to ask me, she went through you."

"You said you didn't want to see her."

"I don't!"

Her grandma let out a hard breath. "I don't understand what the problem is then."

"Neither do I." Annie dropped her head to the table. "I just know when it comes to Jane and Peter, I don't want my life anywhere close."

"Honey." Her grandma patted the back of her head. "You need to let go of whatever it is you're holding on to. It's been years since you and Jane had your falling out."

If it was up to Annie, she'd never have to let it go. Because she'd never have to see Jane and never have to face it. Good thing it was up to Annie and she had that choice. It was tempting to be the bigger woman though. To step in and save the day when Jane was sure Annie was going to let her down. She could parade around that she had saved Jane's ass for the rest of her life. Curse her grandma for playing that card. That was dirty. Dirty and tempting. If only she didn't have to actually do anything for Jane to make that happen. "I'll think about it."

"Thank you—"

"Don't." Annie sat up and pushed hair from her face. "Don't start with the praise. I said I'd think about it, that's all. Honestly, I'm thinking hard about no."

"Thinking is something to hope for. I have your room ready upstairs. I know you've likely had a long day."

She stretched and pushed out of her seat once again. "I'm going to change clothes and head to the bakery."

"Rest up. You don't have to do that today."

"I want to. I want to get a feel for the kitchen again." She smiled at her grandma. She also wanted to get out of this house. In some ways, she'd hoped this would be a happy visit. Make some cupcakes and save the day. Instead, she'd been tricked. The last thing she wanted was to be cooped up here. This house offered more misery than anywhere else in town since they'd lived here before as one big dysfunctional family.

She was the daughter of the slut who'd stolen their dad. She was part of the reason their parents fought, and, by extension, part of the reason their mom died. It wasn't something they liked to let her forget. Tina had thrown more of Annie's toys out a window than she could count, somehow managed to spill water on her homework and was always moving her things. Both of Annie's shoes could be by the door at night, but by the next morning, the right one could be anywhere from buried under dirty clothes to sitting on the back porch. Tina had always seemed hell-bent on intentionally making Annie's life difficult. Jane had been a wild card. It had seemed like if Tina wasn't around, Annie and Jane had been almost friends. At least until Jane had hooked up with Peter.

That had been the final nail Annie had needed to cut ties with Jane like she had with Tina long before. "I know how Grandpa tends to randomly stick things somewhere without having any particular spot."

Her grandma chuckled. "Yeah, you might want to go in and have a look around. The keys are in the car."

Annie slipped on some yoga pants, traded her sandals for tennis shoes and headed out. Fall was one of her favorite seasons of the year. The heat of the summer was gone. Welcomed coolness took its place, and in another month or two, the view would be incredible. The trees coming off the tail end of the Appalachian Mountains would burst with gold and crimson leaves.

She left the quiet neighborhood and headed the few miles past her old high school, on down beyond the empty parking lot that was the place for a teenager to be seen and crossed over into town toward Grandpa's bakery. The town had aged. She slowed down as she came to the intersection at the first red light. A big abandoned building was to the left. That used to be…she racked her brain trying to remember. Something sports or…something. Now the tan metal building had a bit of rust on the outside and the cracked and faded lot in front of it sat empty.

The light turned and she went by three cross streets and took a left at an old familiar red-brick building. *No. 12* was written in concrete across the top, though she'd never known why. It wasn't the address. Grandpa's old *Cookie's Cakes* sign was still over the red and yellow awning.

Annie pulled around to the side of the building. The tires of the car crunched the gravel as she parked near the back door. The key hung from the car key ring and she slid it in the lock. The building was old. The town even older, but the key worked like a charm. She stepped inside and the heavy metal door pounded on the frame and cloaked her in darkness. Even after all the years she'd been gone, everything about this room was clear in her mind. A big table in the middle of the room for all the cakes to be decorated. Oven and refrigerators. Shelves and shelves of storage.

The chair in his office she'd made frequent use of to study books she'd gotten from the library on cakes. Baking them, decorating them, the history of them. Medieval recipes for them. Whatever. If there was a cake on the front of the book, she'd checked it out and generally brought it here. With a snack between them, she'd turned page after page with her grandpa while cakes baked and then cooled. She'd had three amazing years where it had just been her and her grandparents before Jane and Tina's mom had died in that car crash after another fight with their dad. She wasn't sure she should be able to remember things at such a young age, but they were great, happy memories. She didn't have a mom. She didn't have a loving dad. She had her grandparents. Everything about that felt so right and normal and just perfect. It had all changed when Tina and Jane moved in so Dad could travel for work and send money home. Her grandparents had promised her half-sisters were fun.

For a while, Jane had been that sister anyone could ever want. Tina had always been hateful, and it hadn't taken but a few years before she had Jane turn on her. The two had teamed up against Annie—and not just at home either. Nothing big enough to get anyone in any trouble. Enough to annoy Annie. Like taking deodorant out of her gym bag before P.E. Dropping their heavy book bags on hers on the bus so that her lunch would be a squished mess. If they could dream up something to annoy her, they tried it. The teasing had let up when Dad married a woman only six years older than Tina and Mary was born. Thankfully for Mary, she'd gotten to live with Dad and escaped Tina and Jane's wrath when he'd moved away and left his three older girls with his parents.

Annie stepped into the cool room where she'd learned how to weave a basket with frosting, to pipe patterns and perfect the easy art of roses at her grandpa's instructions. The time she'd put in sitting at that little stool making perfect leaves rushed over her and she finally got a little of the warm nostalgia she'd been hoping for.

Even in the dark room, warmth filled her. Not all of Turtle Pine was bad. This place was golden on her list. It was her special place that Tina and Jane hadn't treaded over. She reached to the left and felt along the rough brick wall to the old light switch and flipped it on.

Bright white flickered at first, then powered on strong throughout the long, narrow room. Stainless-steel tables still sat along the center. Old refrigerators were still lined along the left of the room and ovens against the right. She walked down the side, letting her fingers rub against the cool metal as she approached the other end of the room.

Mixes, bowls, measuring cups, icing bags, tips and so much more filled the floor-to-ceiling shelves. That old knee-high wooden ladder Grandpa had put together for her was pushed to the side. She dragged it over, surprising herself at how familiar the thing rocked under her feet and that she remembered how to counter her weight to balance.

With a hand on the shelf, she climbed to the top step and reached the row of pans. There were so many in all sizes. Rounds, squares. A couple specialty animal shapes. Deep ones and trays all sat in their neatly arranged spots. On the end was a set of cupcake pans.

Two of them, to be exact. Annie pulled them out. Forty-eight cupcakes per batch when she had hundreds to go? Not happening. She climbed down with the two pans and went in search of pen and paper. She wasn't staying up all night long baking to deliver fresh cupcakes. She put cupcake pans at the top of her list.

She pulled the heavy refrigerator door open and found what looked like half a pound of butter. The shelf that used to hold the milk was empty. Knowing Grandpa's tendency to rearrange, she pulled open the other refrigerator. Two dozen eggs filled the top shelf, but no milk. She added more to her notes. She was really missing Jared, the food supplier who came through and checked the bakery's stock in Texas on a bi-weekly basis.

The door had long ago been taken off the pantry and she flicked lights on as she stepped into a room that was nearly size of her bedroom. Shelves wrapped most of the walls, but one side was half filled with drawers.

Bags of flour, sugar, baking powder and every other baker's best friend to make cupcakes were gone. Sprinkles though? Grandpa had enough of those you'd think he owned the company who made them. She smiled as she went after a chair. Grandpa always had sprinkles to make every snack better, so she couldn't find too much fault in what she estimated to be fifteen bottles.

She got her hands around the back of a chair just as the hum of something she recognized immediately sounded over the whispering noise of the refrigerators.

Chapter Four

Cade would like to pretend he was driving around aimlessly, but he knew exactly where he was heading as he flicked his blinker on at the stop sign. His odds were fifty-fifty of her being at the bakery. Since the other options for the afternoon were his mom's house with the buzz of wedding-related junk and the nag of his future sister-in law or his house with his neighbor, he rather liked his fifty-fifty chance.

He could always grab a bite to eat, but then he was liable to fall asleep at the table. Call him crazy, but the moment he fell asleep, somehow, Tina would know. It was like the woman had everybody in town with eyes on his back, waiting for the moment she could sweep in and blindside him.

If all else failed, he was hitting a drive-through and going to sit in his deer stand for the day to take a nap. Surely being thirty-five feet up a tree would be enough to escape her.

The tall red brick building was ahead on the right and he didn't want to explain the feeling of relief that filled his chest at the sight of her grandparents' car parked by the back door. He'd wanted to flirt with Annie since the day he'd realized girls didn't have cooties. His brother had swooped in and beaten him to the challenge. The fact that she was two grades ahead of him in school hadn't helped his odds.

When she and his brother had broken up, he'd be lying if he said he hadn't thought about asking her out. Something with her changed though, and it had changed everything about her. There was this vibe all around her. A very strong, very clear *unapproachable* vibe. Annie had turned into the mysterious Annie-Lyn. It had taken him six weeks to get past her cold shoulder to try talking to her in the hall at school. She hadn't broken her power walk, never looked up, and he wasn't certain she'd even heard him. He couldn't even be sure that he'd spoken loud enough over the roar of the noise between classes that she'd even had a chance to hear.

That vibe never left her and he'd never gotten the nerve again.

Even today, there'd been a wall there, but it had come down a little when he'd gotten her out of his truck. He was older, smarter, and the rich sound of her laugh had already gotten under his skin to make him try harder. If nothing else, for the next few days he was going to work hard to hear that sound again. That was if she didn't give him the clear get-away-from-me vibe he tried projecting on Tina.

He pulled in the side lot, wondering for a second if her grandpa was the one actually here. He shrugged it off. The worst that could happen was he'd be given a cookie. That wasn't exactly a bad thing.

Like all the deputies and friends of her grandpa, he walked to the backdoor and gave it a light tap as he twisted the knob and pushed it open. "Knock, knock."

"I guess some things never change." She appeared from a side room. Gone was the fancy dress and back was the girl he remembered. Soft-looking tight pants, a T-shirt and some tennis shoes decked her out as the woman he'd seen at school who'd often carried books tightly against her chest.

Except this time, she was minus the cold shoulder. Her smile was all warm and inviting. Shoulders back, hair lose around her face, she searched him. Whew. There went his pulse.

His throat got extra tight and he forced himself to swallow so his voice wouldn't crack. Even though he was older, those teenage nerves rushed back over him. At the airport, she'd been cold and shut off. But this woman was all smiles and focused on him without giving him some warm-up time. "Don't change what's working."

She placed a notebook on the table in the center of the room and sat on a stool. "Are you following me today or is this just coincidence?"

"Some of both?" He shrugged, hooked a chair by his foot and dragged it up to sit opposite her. Might as well throw some of this out in the open. "I'm hiding from my neighbor."

"Not a good sign about your neighborhood."

"It has its pluses and minuses." Mostly minuses. Since Tina had run him out of his house today, and he was out looking for Annie because of it, that could be considered a plus. "What about where you live?"

"Apartment building where I'm loved by everyone on my floor." A light chuckle came out of her.

"That doesn't surprise me." She must give her neighbors the warm smile more often than the cold shoulder.

"I bring a lot of day-old items home. People love snacks."

"Would be a sin not to." He gestured at the notebook. "Making a list?"

"Trying to figure out supplies. Grandpa's scraping the barrel here since he hasn't been in the bakery."

Welp, it'd been, oh, a good ten or fifteen years since he'd gotten up the nerve to ask her out. This time she was actually looking at him, so his odds had to be better. Of course, that meant if she said no, he'd have no excuses for the refusal this time. He rubbed his sweaty-as-hell palms over his thighs. "You about done with that?"

She blinked and sat back. "Just started, why?"

"Thought you might want to take a ride around town. Get a feel for the place again. This is your first time back since you left, isn't it?"

Her grin somehow deepened and she placed the pen across the top of the notebook. Her tongue darted out to wet her lips and disappeared again. "It is. Has it changed a bunch since I left?"

"Well, they repainted the water tower."

She gasped and dramatically covered her chest with her hand. "They took off *Jeremy + Melissa*?"

"They did. Someone went up and painted it back the first night after they were done." Being Jeremy was pushing sixty-five, everyone agreed he wasn't the culprit, but any one of his rowdy grandkids had a lot of potential. Cade had been tasked with figuring out which one had defaced the new paint, but he hadn't put a lot of effort into it. The mayor had been the one who'd wanted the tower painted and everyone knew that was only because Melissa had picked Jeremy over him. *Jeremy + Melissa* on that water tower was a part of Turtle Pine history. You just can't paint over history.

She laughed. "You're kidding."

"Nope."

She was laughing more. "I don't think it would feel like home if it wasn't there."

"I think almost everybody thought the same. You remember Mrs. Baxter?"

She frowned for a moment and stared at the center of the table. "She has the big rose bushes behind her mailbox."

He pointed. "Used to have. She pulled them up."

Annie's mouth dropped. "No."

"Yep."

"Those bushes have been there for as long as I can remember. And I remember her being out there all the time trimming on them."

"Gone. She ripped them up. Shocked everybody."

She leaned on the counter, meaning she leaned toward him. "I'd probably get lost on the way to the school without seeing those bushes at the corner."

"My point exactly." He pointed at her list again. "So are you about done? We're burning daylight."

She thumbed through the sheets of mostly empty paper. "I guess the rest can wait. Not like I'm calling in an order tonight."

"Perfect. And I have a surprise for you."

"Surprises already?" The raise of her brow was full of skepticism.

Nice. Way to come off looking creepy. He slipped his hands in his pockets to rub off even more sweat from his palms. "It was something I had to do, so it wasn't just for you. But the benefit is still the same."

She flicked the lights off and turned the lock as she followed him out the door. "I'm almost afraid."

"You shouldn't be." He pulled the door closed, gave a push and a tug to make sure it had caught. He pointed to his cleaned-up truck. The paint was too old and sun-faded to be considered shiny and looking like new, but it was clean. "Washed her all up for you."

"Oh." She blinked and stared. "You sure did." Then she frowned.

No. Don't frown. "Something wrong?"

"I hope you don't think I was offended by the dirt earlier."

"No, I've just had girls not want to get in when it's muddy before."

"Prissy girls, sounds like." She stopped and faced him with a slight narrowing of her eyes. "Do you think I'm prissy?"

"I never thought you were, I mean, I don't want you to think that. I didn't want to ruin any of your things." In his rambling, he caught her smile out the corner of his eye. "There's no winning this conversation, is there?"

"Not really. I'm just teasing you. But honestly, it was fine the way it was." She tugged open the door before he could get it, and pulled her way up on the seat as efficiently as she had before. "You sound like you get it muddy a lot."

He started his truck. "Depends on what the teenagers do on the weekends. They know not to go riding on Bryan Neuimer's land, but when there's a good, hard rain, they take off. Neuimer calls the department and I get sent out to find them."

She turned in the seat and faced him a little like she did before. "So basically, when the kids go out, you get paid to ride around in the woods."

He grinned and nodded. "Pretty much."

"Nice. Sounds like the perfect job."

"I would have thought yours was. You get paid to eat cupcakes."

She laughed. "Okay, that's true. My job is pretty awesome like that, but I don't know. I think you have me beat. It's hard to top mud riding."

He tried imagining the girl he remembered in his truck when the tires were slinging mud. Image didn't fit. "I would have never thought you were big into mud riding."

"I was probably its biggest fan."

He flashed her a grin and couldn't help teasing her a little. "I remember you being the biggest book nerd around."

She laughed. The sound carried over the rumble of the engine and the roar of the tires. "That's true. Books were my ticket out of town. If I hadn't quit mud riding to study, goodness knows where I'd be."

He wanted to point out that he'd noticed she'd become a book nerd after his brother had started dating her sister, but to do that meant she'd likely get either pissed or upset. He'd liked to avoid both. "Books took you all the way to college and into a bakery far, far away."

"Yeah, they did. College gave me a marketing degree."

"I would have thought a baking degree."

She laughed. "They don't have those degrees at your standard university, and I didn't get in a culinary school. Besides, I already knew how to bake. I had a knack for decorating. I needed to learn how to run a business. While I was in school, I got to intern at this amazing bakery. They bake huge cakes and ship them all over the country. Sometimes they fly to different states to put them together."

"Sounds like something I've watched on TV."

She nodded. "Yeah, like those. It's that kind of nationwide amazing bakery. I did a good job. After my internship was over, they hired me on part-time to help with things like standard storefront snacks. Then I slowly worked my way in full-time doing that. Eventually, an opportunity came up where I got to assist on a custom cake. Then another and another. And now I'm taking on my own custom orders. It's really cool."

"Living the dream?"

"I am." Her smile was broad and her eyes focused on him.

He cleared his throat again and made a point to watch the road so he didn't stare at her and run them in the ditch. "No desire to open your own bakery anymore?"

She lifted a shoulder. "Sometimes I think about that. The bakery I work for is amazing, but of course I don't run it, so there are things I would do a little different here and there. Overall though, I'm completely happy and have no plans to leave."

He turned at the stop sign and she moaned. The sound pricked all his nerve endings and he nearly shuddered. "Everything okay?"

She faced him with this pleading expression all over her face. "Jasper's." She shook her head. "One of the hardest parts about leaving. You can't find cheeseburgers and milkshakes anywhere like what they serve."

He flicked on his blinker and pulled in the front lot. "Jasper's it is."

"You don't have to. I can stop by later."

"I'm hungry anyway." And like hell was he passing up this opportunity. Taking Annie to Jasper's for burgers and milkshakes? He'd wanted this to happen more times than he could count. He pulled the keys from the engine and got out before she had a chance to try and talk him out of it.

She reached for the door and stopped. "I left my purse at the bakery. We'll need to go back."

"Nah." He pushed his door closed. He was not getting back in the Jeep and missing this chance. "It's on me."

She hopped out. "I'll pay you back."

"Or you can buy it next time."

"Deal." She grinned as she reached his side.

She didn't lean into him and wrap an arm around his waist like he'd always pictured, but he did get the chance to pull the door open and let her walk in ahead of him. She paused after she stepped in the old building and inhaled deeply. "Oh, man. Smell hasn't changed."

"I don't think the burgers have changed either."

"Good."

He ordered a couple of burgers, fries and two shakes to top it off. "Pick your table."

She went to the perfect table located in a back corner next to a front window. It was a little private and had some late afternoon sunshine. She rubbed over the top of her thighs as she settled in the booth. "Funny how I've been gone so long but nothing is really that different."

"Nobody likes change."

"I guess. I suppose I imagined to come back, be older and not recognize things. Or see it different, but it's the same." She plucked a couple napkins out and spread one over her lap. "So other than being a mud-riding deputy, what else are you up to these days?"

Mostly hiding from her sisters, but he didn't want to mention any of that. "Not too much. Staying busy with work."

"I wouldn't think you'd have a whole lot to do in a small town. Speeding tickets?"

"Every now and then. It's really the teenagers who keep me busy. Everyone wants to throw a party with beer and not get caught."

"I see." Her head tipped to the side. "No women in your life?"

"Just my mom."

She chuckled.

Paula eased by their table with a tray and unloaded their food. She did a double take on Annie. "Annie Cookie?"

She smiled. "Hi, Paula."

"I heard you were coming." She bent over. "Give me a hug."

Annie reached up from her seat and embraced the woman. "Cade was taking me through town to get a feel of the place again and I saw the diner is still here. I've been missing your burgers since the day I left. I had no idea you'd be in during the evening though."

"I flipped to the evening shift years ago. If you hadn't stayed gone so long, you'd know that."

She nodded. "I know. Grandma already gave me the run-through."

"I've been seeing your pretty cakes on the Instagram. Beautiful work. I was pleased as punch when I heard you were coming back to bake all those cupcakes for the kids."

"Grandpa already promised them before the first game, and you know how he hates to disappoint. I'm happy I get to do it."

Paula shifted her weight into one leg. "Rumor is you're doing your sister's wedding cake."

Annie's smile got a little tight. "I've heard that rumor too."

Paula laughed and swatted her with their meal ticket. "That's my girl. Good luck with that. Let me get going before Jasper gets his tail in a knot."

Paula eased off and Cade chuckled. "You two seem close."

Annie lifted a shoulder and salted her fries. "A little. It was usually loud at the house in the afternoon, so when the library was closed and I needed a quiet place to study, Paula let me use the store room in the back."

"I never knew that."

She rearranged a few fries and kept talking without looking at him. "It was nice. Paula and I have a lot in common."

"You have a lot in common with a woman twice your age who didn't make it past tenth grade?"

She nodded. "Yeah." She squirted ketchup and opened and closed her mouth a few times. Something was on the verge of coming out, but she wouldn't let it. A puddle of ketchup went on her plate and she blew out a breath. "Her mom ran out on her too."

Annie put the ketchup back in the center of the table and still didn't look up. Cade treaded carefully because he knew very little about Annie's parents. He knew she was only a half-sister to Jane and Tina. By the timing of Annie's and Jane's birthday, their dad had been sneaking around with Annie's mom while his wife had been pregnant with Jane. It was one of those things nobody talked about, but somehow everybody knew about it. "That can't be easy with her gone. Have you ever tried contacting her?"

"No. Grandma said my mom didn't know Dad was married when they were together and just wanted out. She'd planned to give me up for adoption, but Grandma and Grandpa stepped in. Dad was busy trying to fix his marriage to Tina and Jane's mom, so he wasn't in any sort of mindset to think about me. Or so I heard."

And then fast-forward to years later to Jane stealing Annie's boyfriend. It was all one big messed-up circle. He couldn't blame Annie for wanting out.

"So." She breathed and brushed her fingertips. "That's my dirty laundry. Tell me something happy before the rest of this day turns into a massive downer."

He grinned her way. "I always thought you were the most beautiful girl I'd ever seen."

Her smile was back. "Flattery will get you everywhere."

"Good to know." He ate a fry. "Has anyone told you that you have the best laugh?"

She snorted. "How did you turn into such a handful?"

"I read a lot."

"Interesting."

He lifted a shoulder. "Not too much. The prettiest girl I knew moved away from town and left me with nothing to do."

She laughed some more. If only she knew how much of that was true. Somewhat. He did read a lot. And he'd started reading when she left. Not because he was pining after her—though perhaps that had been part of it—he'd wanted to know what had fascinated her so much. Turned out, books were pretty damn fun, so he'd kept reading.

The burgers and fries were gone in a flash and she sat back in the booth with a happy moan while she poked her straw in her shake. "That was wonderful. Thank you, but I'm afraid you may have to wheel me out of here now."

"You'll have to take me first."

"Sounds like my tour of the town is over."

He arched backward, reaching his arms overhead and a couple of satisfying pops went through his back. "Maybe I have a second wind in me. We haven't looped around the other side of town to see the water tower yet."

"Can't forget that. I can't wait to see what color they made it."

"An ugly blue."

She blinked. "Blue?"

"Yep."

"Why blue?"

"I have no idea." He chuckled and eased out of his booth.

He extended his hand to her before he thought different about it. Not that there was any reason he shouldn't hold out his hand to help her out of the booth, but hand touching was more date-like. And this wasn't a date, was it? Then she went and slipped her hand in his and he stopped caring about what this was.

As he tugged her out of that booth and she ended up standing with her toes nearly touching his, this could be anything he wanted. For the moment, he wanted this to be a date. It was easy to believe as she lifted her gaze to his.

He could nearly read his own thoughts in her eyes. He should pull his hand away. Or something. Where was this going, really? Nowhere. Or well…it was also going right into something he'd spent years daydreaming about.

In all those daydreams, he'd pulled her from that booth and walked her to the door with his hand still holding hers. So that's exactly what he did.

"Let's get out of here before it gets late."

She nodded, opened her mouth for a moment and then closed it. She smiled and let out a soft chuckle. "Yeah, okay."

When her eyes landed back on his, they were no longer searching. That uncertainty that had mirrored his own seemed gone. Just what had gone through her head in the two-point-five seconds that had ended with a quick head shake and a laugh? He was afraid to ask and risk changing her mind.

Because that was the kind of look from her he'd wanted to see. Trusting. Ready to go. He lead her out the door and around to the passenger side of his truck. He pulled the door open and started to grab her waist to help her up, but like before, she got the handle and slid on the high seat like she did it every day.

He got in behind the wheel and left Jasper's. "So I'm thinking a swing around the north side and that'll cover the town."

"You've done a great job."

"Not over yet." He pulled out and headed around the opposite side of town, pointing out small changes that had taken place here and there. He enjoyed her smile as she pointed at the playground and then mentioned houses she used to walk past on her way home from school. The shake of her head at the water tower that stuck out like a sore thumb.

He turned down another street that brought them back through town and finally back to the parking lot at the bakery. "Thanks for going along for the ride."

"Thank you for taking me. It was—" she let out a breath and looked around the nearby buildings, "—it was good. To see it all again, but from someone else's point of view."

He got comfortable with a hand over the steering wheel. "How so?"

"Everything I guess. You looked at the school and had good memories. I look and I don't really remember it that way at first. I have to think back."

"You seemed focused at school."

She laughed. "I was."

"Hard to have too much fun with that kind of focus."

She glanced his way and an eyebrow went up. "You'd be surprised what happens when people forget you're there."

"I don't believe you."

"It's true. I've seen girls cheating on boyfriends. Boys taking advantage of their friends' younger sisters while they giggled along. Supposedly *best* friends saying the worst things about each other behind their backs."

"No, I mean about people forgetting about you. I don't believe that."

She blinked at him as her cheeks stained red. She rubbed the tops of her thighs and cleared her throat. "Well, maybe I wasn't as invisible as I always thought. Maybe they just didn't care."

"Or you didn't see the right people noticing."

She licked her lips. "Or maybe that too." She breathed out. "I need to take off. Grandpa was down at Mark's when I got home and I haven't seen him yet."

"Don't forget to tip your guide."

She chuckled and got out. "That reminds me, I need to grab my purse."

He stepped out and met her at the front of the truck as she came around it.

"You didn't have to get out. I'm sure you probably have a hundred things to do today."

All of them involved avoiding his neighbor. "Always walk a pretty girl to the door."

She blushed again. He liked seeing that color in her cheeks. It brightened her up. As much as she wanted to talk about blending into the shadows and disappearing, she'd never be able to pull it off, not as long as that color was brightening her face. She tucked hair behind her ear and slid her key into the lock.

He stepped inside with her as she flicked on the overhead lights. This was only the second time he'd ever been in this room when it was still cool. So much so that a chill went over his spine before he even thought of it.

The move caught her gaze. "You're cold?"

He chuckled. "Not really. I'm used to this room being hot."

She stared at him and they were secluded with the door latching shut behind him. That quick shiver left him far behind and was replaced by warmth filling his veins.

"It's the ovens. About the only time the heater comes on is in the winter when Grandpa first gets here in the morning."

"And when he sits around the table for coffee with all his buddies."

She laughed and nodded. "Then too. I guess I thought maybe they didn't do that anymore, since Grandma said he was down at Mark's drinking coffee."

"From what I understand, it's only because the bakery is closed because of his wrist. He manages a few snacks at home and then they congregate at Mark's."

"After they get in that habit of being surrounded by cars at Mark's shop, it'll be a miracle if he comes back and reopens."

"Lot of people are going to be disappointed if the bakery closes. You can get three square meals a day here."

She laughed and lifted her purse. "That was something I always wanted to add to my bakery." She glanced to him. "Actual meals. Not donuts for breakfast and cake for lunch and supper."

He eased closer. Everything about her pulled him in like magnets. He could hang out here, listening to her talk about her dreams for hours. "What's that?"

"Sandwiches." She lifted a shoulder and fumbled with the straps. "There's stuff already here for breakfast and snacks. The middle of the day is wide open with no need to bring customers in, but you're here working anyway because you're baking for that after school and evening crowd. So why not add some loaves of fresh bread to sell? And then cut some of that bread for quick sandwiches. More than likely, people will at least buy a cookie while they're here too, so you sell more of your baked things anyway."

He would live here. Jaspers was great, but too much of it and it was like he moved in slow-motion. Being he spent most his time running after teenagers with a metabolism through the roof, slow-motion wasn't a good idea. "Does the place you work at do that?"

"Nah. They have a stable of select sweets for the front of the store and then custom-order cakes and stuff. They don't even make bread. But they're really busy. They're in a big city with a steady stream of customers coming in for what they want. I don't think they could handle the additional traffic if they added lunch options."

"I guess you'll have to move back home and take over here so your grandpa can keep hanging out at Mark's. Then you get your dream too." As soon as he said the words, the idea filled his head and he liked what he saw. Which was about the most ridiculous thought to have. They'd had one date—if this could even be counted as a date. He was certainly counting it, but this was more than counting chickens before they'd hatched. Having those kinds of ideas was also counting eggs before they'd even been laid. But, man, it made for a nice thought.

She laughed. The sound was heavy and full and something he was starting to crave.

"Yeah, I don't think so."

Even knowing it was never going to happen, the disappointment was still heavy. "I figured it was a longshot."

"So long that I can't even see the other end. There's no way I could ever come back home."

Rough. She was slowly killing him. "You're never tempted to come back?"

She caught her lip between her teeth as her gaze strayed around the room. "I would be lying if I said I hadn't ever thought about it. I love my grandparents. And I miss them, but…"

"But…"

She lifted a shoulder. "You know the history between me and my sisters. I escaped all that and I don't want to live near them."

So she was letting them chase her off and dictate her life. He kept that to himself because he didn't know Annie well enough to throw stuff like that around. "I guess my only hope then is that I change your mind."

She lightly chuckled, but the sound died as she was back to searching him like in the diner. "Cade…that's—"

He put his finger over her mouth and her words ended at his fingertip. He didn't want to hear confirmation that she was leaving. He knew that. Obviously, she was only here temporarily. For now though? He liked the idea of this. He liked the idea of living out an old dream. He wanted to know if this could be better than what he'd ever imagined.

He moved his finger. His name was a whisper. A gasp filled the otherwise quiet room and hesitant lips touched his. He leaned in closer, sliding his hand along her cheek and tipping her chin to his. Her soft lips parted and she hesitated for a breath. He started to pull away, but she moved against his.

In the way he had always pictured, the kiss was slow but full of everything he'd always wanted it to be—only it was clouded by the uncertainty about what this was, what it could mean, what it could lead to. He knew exactly what he wanted, but a quick fling with her while she was in town for a few days wasn't it. He wanted to get to know her. See if she'd changed. See if she was more than the woman he'd always imagined her.

He wanted so much more. Her taste in his memory. Her opening to him. Her hand coming up his arm like it currently was. The soft sigh humming from the back of her throat.

She was sweet, tempting him for more. She made him want everything and more than anything he'd ever thought of. She fisted her hands in his shirt. In his dreams, she opened the row of buttons down the front of him.

This shirt didn't have buttons though. He also wasn't an anxious fifteen-year-old anymore. He'd waited this long to kiss her. He could wait longer before hopefully anything else. He pressed his lips to hers one last time and pulled away.

"I'll see you around."

She blinked and nodded. "Yeah. See you." She flicked hair out of her eyes. "Around."

He eased out the door while she watched him go. She blindly touched over the table in the center of the room, patting in different places as though she was looking for something. He stepped outside into the late afternoon sun with her taste and smell filling him.

Chapter Five

Well, yeah, Annie had had boyfriends since Peter. She'd for sure kissed boys too. Lots of them. Okay, not lots. But enough. None of them had ever swept her off her feet like Cade just had. Of course, she'd always been so focused and driven by work and school and often balancing them both that she hadn't exactly left a lot of room in her life for romance.

She touched her lips, wishing she could still feel him, but he was gone. He'd somehow come out of nowhere and caught her right when she didn't have a lot of things to juggle. Her hands were, for the most part, free. And those free hands wanted to get back on his arms. And do more to his shirt besides grab it. Piling all his clothes on the floor seemed like a great idea.

She shook her head to get her thoughts out of the clouds. The cupcakes might be a cakewalk of a job, and she did have a lot of time on her hands while waiting for supplies to come in before she could start baking. Still, there wasn't time for all that. Well, okay, so there was time, literal time, for Cade, but she didn't really *have time* for him. Because to spend time with him was a distraction. She didn't have distractions in Turtle Pine.

This place was a quick stop of a trip only. In and out as fast as time allowed. She waved her hands in front of her face, wishing it was as easy as that to clear her thoughts. It wasn't, and she grabbed her purse and locked the door as she went out it.

Problem was, she'd never had down time while here. Not since before Peter and Jane got together. She'd always had a drive that burned inside. A purpose with a clear goal at the end of the tunnel to stay completely focused on.

Now though, there was nothing but waiting until she got her supplies together and called the supplier. Which couldn't happen until tomorrow. And after that? Back to twiddling her thumbs until the delivery truck arrived. Hopefully the next day. Good Lord, what if she didn't get a delivery until Thursday? She sank behind the wheel of her grandma's car. What in the heck was she going to do with herself between now and when the delivery truck got here?

She dropped her head back. Even if the delivery truck came on Tuesday, that would mean she had nothing to occupy her time until Thursday morning. As much as she wanted something on her hands, she was only delivering the freshest cupcakes possible to the school. Her best option to keep her hands busy was Jane's wedding cake. And she most certainly was not doing that. Annie backed from the spot and headed back to Grandma's. As good as that kiss with Cade had been, it wasn't the best idea to spend her time making out with him when she was leaving town by the end of the week.

Or spend any time making out with him really. Because…of reasons.

That's all she knew. *Reasons*. It didn't need to be any more specific than that, did it? She was only here temporarily. He knew that. He might be fine with that. And she was probably okay with a little temporary fun distraction herself. They were both consenting adults.

Still. Reasons. Yeah, she'd stick with that and not look too much further into it. She parked in front of the old house and spotted her grandpa sitting in the rocking chair on the porch.

As she let out a breath, she loosened her grip around the steering wheel. Guilt trip number two lay just ahead. Might as well get it over with. With any luck, she'd manage it without being double-teamed by both of them since Grandma wasn't outside.

By the time she got out of the car, Grandpa had stood up on the porch. She came up the steps and met him there with a tight hug. The usual smell of sugar and baking and treats was gone, and oil and motor-like things were in their place.

Flour that usually dusted the front of him was replaced by grease spots. "Enjoying your time out of the bakery?"

"Mark was showing me something on a '72 Camaro and it sputtered a bit."

"Glad you're making the most of your time off."

"Trying to."

"How's your hand feeling?" She eased into a rocking chair next to him.

He lifted his arm and turned it over, showing her the blue strapped-on cast. Like his shirt, it was smeared with grease and oil and probably a few other things. "Nothing more than a nuisance now."

"That's good to hear. Hopefully, you'll have that thing off in no time."

"Doctor says I got a few more weeks. Your grandma said you were going to the bakery?"

"I did. Looks a lot like I remembered. I'll need to place a food order. Grandma said you had a number I could call?"

He nodded. "It's at the bakery on the cork board on a scratch piece of paper. Some five-nine number or something."

"I'm sure I'll find it." Likely around the hundred other pieces of paper attached to the board. Eventually, the right person had to answer. "You're scraping the barrel of stuff up there."

His gray, bushy brows lifted. "Yeah. Your grandma froze a lot of the milk and we've been using it. We ate the eggs. I'd heard you went down to Jasper's with Cade, so I didn't know if you made it over to the bakery or not."

What was that heat filling her cheeks like a blush about? She rubbed her neck. "He picked me up at the airport earlier."

"I thought Tina was supposed to do that?"

"Long story. Cade got me instead."

He all but rolled his eyes. A move that never failed to make her smile. "That girl. I don't know what to do with her. Don't listen to nobody. Can't tell her nothing. Making a fool of herself going on like she does."

While Grandma liked to be nice and not talk about anybody in the family, Grandpa told it like it was. They spent a lot of time in the bakery together and his filter concerning the family was nonexistent when it came to her.

But Annie would stay out of that one, how Tina was making a fool of herself and any other thing relating her sisters. In and out of Turtle Pine. That's what Annie was about. "When is Mary coming in? Or at least, I'm guessing she'll be in for the wedding? With Dad?"

He nodded. "Late Friday or sometime Saturday, I heard."

"Oh. Hate that. I guess I'll miss her. And them." They weren't close, but Mary hadn't been mean to her. Annie didn't really know her younger sister well. She was only about sixteen or so. Annie hated to leave the poor girl on her own against Tina and Jane, but Mary would have Dad and her mom here with her, so she wouldn't have it too hard. Those two wouldn't say a mean thing to Mary so long as Dad was around. Why he deserved their undying love, she hadn't figured that part out. He'd cheated on their mom. Had another baby with another woman. Dumped them all off in their grandparents' laps and they rarely saw or heard from him after he'd run off and married a different young girl and started himself up a whole new family.

For Tina and Jane, it made perfect sense to love and adore him and hate the sister that was always standing right there.

Mercy. *In and out.*

"Your grandma mentioned you didn't want to do Jane's wedding cake."

There was the bomb. *Pcka-whaaa.* The explosion echoed through her head. While the dust settled, she shored up to sitting straight in her chair. "I really don't want to."

"All right."

That was it? He just smiled at her. She swallowed the bucket-sized knot in her throat and considered her words careful. This felt like a trick. Or someone was about to hop out from the bushes with a camera and reveal the real response. "I hope you're not disappointed."

"Not too disappointed, but not surprised either."

Ouch. That stung. Nothing like one of your favorite people in the whole world telling you they're not surprised to be disappointed in you. "I don't think it would be a good idea."

He crossed his fingers over his belly and let out a low breath. "I told your grandma that when she said you'd do it."

"You…" Grandma's idea. Little pieces to this puzzle were starting to float together.

"I told her you wouldn't want to do it, but you know your grandma.

Tina takes after her a little bit with that head of hers."

Annie chuckled. "She was determined to change my mind earlier."

"She'll be digging at your heels so long as you're here. When are you leaving?"

"Sometime Sunday morning. That's when the next flight home is. I'll have the cupcakes wrapped up Friday."

He was quiet for several moments. The birds chirped and she enjoyed the companionable, comfortable silence. This was how life was supposed to turn out. This rocking-chair moment was the stuff she'd dreamed up as a kid.

He tipped his head to the side and glanced her way from the corner of his eyes. "I don't blame you for not wanting to do the cake."

She smiled his way. "Thanks."

"When your grandma was telling Jane she was going to get you to do it, Jane didn't think you would either. Jane told her over and over they were fine and would find someone else."

Well, it was good to know Jane still wasn't the self-centered girl Annie remembered. Before the idea even came up in her head to question other ways Jane might have changed, Annie shut it down. *In and out.* "I'm glad she has other options."

"I told her she better make plans for one. Neither of us thought it'd be a good idea to throw that in your lap. Worst-case scenario is we'd end up with an extra cake."

"Not much of a downside."

"No, it ain't." He chuckled and sat back in his chair. "No, it ain't, at all."

Annie picked at the dried varnish flaking off the old wooden armrests. "Where did she manage to get one at the last minute?"

"Sam's Grocery over in Spearsville. Not what she wanted, but said she isn't getting married for cake."

Well, that was very big of Jane. "Where is Grandma?"

"Went to pick up some barbeque for supper. She's claiming she's too upset over Jane's wedding cake to cook." He lightly chuckled and glanced her way. "You might want to make plans to eat somewhere else."

Annie dropped her head against the rocking chair. "I guess I'll have to face the music eventually."

"You might want to wait to face it until tomorrow after she's had a night of sleep. Maybe then she won't be so keyed up."

Or she'll sleep on it and be worse. "I think I might head back to the bakery and finish making my list of supplies. I didn't get done with that earlier. Or I'll go to Jasper's and catch up with Paula. I really need to do both."

"Your grandma will be back any minute now, so if you're going, you better get."

She pushed out of the chair knowing full well she was running, but she didn't really care. "Thanks. I'll be back later this evening sometime."

She headed across town. She started for the bakery but went to Jasper's first. A large Vanilla Coke was exactly what she wanted for the afternoon to figure the math to know how many pounds of everything to buy. And some cheese tater-tots.

Maybe she could even stretch this evening out further with a trip through the grocery store. Few eggs, a couple pounds of flour and sugar, and she was nothing but a little bit of work away from a pan of brownies.

But first, her Vanilla Coke. She parked at Jasper's and barely made it through the front door before Paula was on her. "Well, look at you go. Been in town a couple hours and already picking up Turtle Pine's most eligible and robbing the cradle at the same time."

"What?" Oh, like she didn't know though. At least she knew the picking-up part. Most eligible bachelor though? That sounded like some juicy news that she shouldn't care about. But she totally did.

"Cade Revlin."

"Please. And even if I was—which I'm not—he was only two years behind me in school."

"*Mmm hmm.*" Paula eyed her and didn't look to be believing her one bit. "Well, if you're not serious, you better watch your step. His mom is on a mission to see him married off."

Annie laughed and wouldn't address that flittering dancing across her skin. "Why?"

Paula shrugged. "Moms worry, I guess. He's in his thirties. Never really had a serious girlfriend."

Annie found that hard to believe. With the way he flirted with her, he sounded like he could have any woman he wanted. "Maybe he hasn't found a girl he likes enough."

"Until now." Paula lifted a brow. "He's also being looked at to take his dad's place as sheriff one day. A wife and baby would look pretty next to him if he was campaigning."

"That's a horrible reason to marry someone."

"I never said it was a great reason, but you two would make pretty babies. That's a good reason."

She laughed. Paula was impossible, but Cade never having a serious girlfriend before was interesting. It shouldn't be since that's not what she was in town for, but it was because the nothing-serious part echoed her dating life. Guys came in the bakery. She flirted. They flirted. They went out some, but it wasn't wonderful. It was just okay. Going out on four or five dates with the same guy didn't give off sparks like the few minutes she'd spent with Cade this afternoon—not including that kiss. Paula was looking at her, looking like she could read her thoughts. "Stop, it's not like that. I haven't even been home a day and I'm leaving as soon as I can."

"If I was your age, I'd move hell and high water to make it that way." A plate appeared off the bar from the kitchen. Paula plucked the ticket off the side and grabbed the plate. "Let me drop this off real quick."

Annie fixed her drink and settled on the old bar stool that sat the exact same way as she remembered it years ago. There was a little creak as she found a comfortable spot. A little twist as she adjusted on the uneven padding so it was tolerable. She shook the ice loose in her cup as Paula came back around the corner.

Paula rested a hand on her hip. "So what's it like between you and Cade then?"

"Nothing. He just showed me around town."

"Uh-huh." Paula arched a brow. "It's not too often Cade takes a woman out to dinner."

"He probably didn't plan to this time. I mentioned coming here. Plus, I'll be out of here next Sunday."

Paula frowned. "So fast?"

Annie took a quick and serious interest in pushing the pop bubbles of her drink lid in. "I think the quicker the better."

"I think you ought to stay. If for nothing else than so your sister can get married all the while knowing you're in town and refusing to do her cake."

Annie snorted. "I'll avoid the drama."

"That doesn't leave you much time to fall in love with Cade so you'll move back home."

"Also avoiding that."

"You're avoiding a lot. Some habits don't change, do they?"

Ouch. Nail on the head. It was true and it shouldn't sting, but Paula was right. Some habits most certainly didn't change. This wasn't just about a habit though. This was survival. "It's for the best."

"Not sure I agree with that, but I'm glad you're not doing the cake. Most people said you would cave and do it. I said you wouldn't, so I'm winning right now."

Winning? Oh crap. "Don't tell me there's a bet going on whether or not I'm making a cake."

"Okay. So I won't tell you there's one." Paula just gave her a look. "You know that book is sitting on Becket's counter right now, like it always is. As soon as we heard you were coming, it went down and people started naming odds. I came out first and said you weren't." She leaned in and lowered her voice. "Your grandpa said you weren't doing that cake either, but he didn't want your grandma to know he was betting against her, so he's using a fake name."

Anybody would spot a fake name in the book. There weren't enough people living in town to pass that off. "I guess it's not too surprising people are betting I would since most people don't know Jane and I still don't talk. I hope you have a good payout coming."

"Last I saw it was up to a hundred and fifty." She eyed Annie. "I hope you haven't been telling a lot of people that you're leaving on Sunday. There's still a couple more days left for some money to be put down."

"Just you and Grandpa." And maybe Cade. "According to Grandpa, Grandma has her sights set on changing my mind."

"That's a set of crosshairs I wouldn't want any part of."

"Ditto." She eased off the stool. Speaking of Grandma, she was likely already back at the house, and that meant it was close to supper time. Which meant Jasper's was about to be packed, and that was something else Annie didn't want any part of.

"Going already?"

"I need to swing by the grocery store and stop by the bakery tonight."

"All right. If I see Cade tonight, I'll let him know you're probably there." She grinned. "All *alone*."

"Don't get ideas in your head."

"Just try and stop me." Paula straightened. "Oops. Too late. Ninety percent of the time I see him in here for supper, so be ready to see him later."

"Yeah, yeah. Wasting your time and his."

"I'll take that risk. Can I talk you into making me some brownies? I love your brownies."

Annie chuckled. "Even though you're being a pain in the butt, I suppose I can."

Paula grinned. "Make sure you have enough leftovers. Cade likes brownies too."

Annie was going to need a bigger pan of brownies.

And not because she planned to share them. Maybe. Probably not.

Reasons. There were reasons why she shouldn't share. Like it was a waste of her time and feelings. She wasn't moving back home. Cade was being groomed to take over for sheriff, so he wasn't leaving Turtle Pine. If that wasn't the biggest reason out there, then strap the bracelets on her and haul her off to the looney bin.

Chapter Six

Cade released his blinds and stepped back from the windows. He'd managed to dodge Tina on the way in. On the way out, she was making it a different story. For the last twenty minutes, Tina had piddled around outside. She'd watered flowers. Filled birdfeeders. *Dusted* wind chimes. Who dusted wind chimes?

He didn't want to see what else she might have in mind to clean. He'd been on the other side of the county most of yesterday and by the time he'd come back through, Annie had been gone from the bakery. They weren't in any sort of drop-by-her-grandparents-house relationship, so he hadn't seen her. He'd gotten off work an hour ago. It was already closing in on four, and if he didn't go right now, he was going to miss Annie again.

He grabbed his keys and prepared to sprint to his truck to skirt by with only a wave to Tina. He made it as far as behind the wheel and even managed to get the door closed, but with the open top, that was as far as he got before she was by his side with a rag in her hands.

She smiled his way. "You're in a hurry."

"I've got a few things to do."

She just nodded and didn't move. "Do you think you'll be back later?"

"I'm sure I will be at some point." Unless he moved today. That wasn't likely.

She chuckled and put her hand on his truck door. Rested there. "Of course. I meant early. I've got a box of fall decorations that I can't get down. I've wiggled it and tried lifting and I swear the thing is nailed to the shelf."

Crap. And what the hell? She had a teenager. Who flipped tires for football practice. Smelled like bullshit. "Pat can't budge it either? He mentioned he's been working out with the football team."

She grinned. "He's tried. I think he's still a little weak from the antibodies and stuff. Jane planned to borrow a few things to decorate the tables at the wedding."

Cornered, but he wasn't going to risk missing Annie. "If I don't get back in time tonight, I'll get it before the weekend. Tomorrow I'll be out of town with work for most of the day." Because he was back on patrol in that part of the county.

"Thank you." She tipped her head to the side as she uttered the words and slowly backed away. "You're such a sweetheart to me. I appreciate it."

"No problem." He backed out and rubbed his arm over the truck where she'd been resting. He got across town for a drive-by of the bakery. Luck finally got on his side, the car Annie had been driving was parked there. He stopped next to her and gave a quick call to Peter for the man to go collect his own decorations for his wedding. If Tina managed to get Cade in her house, he may never make it back out alive.

With that off his mind, he hopped out and moved a little faster at the sweet scent in the air. Was she baking the cupcakes for Friday already? It was only Tuesday. He pulled open the door and found her sitting on a stool. Country music filled the air and bowls were set around the counter. More were on a rack off to the side. Trays were pretty well covering every other available surface. From being in here with her grandpa, he knew there should be something cooling in those pans on the rack.

She sat up and stretched her arms overhead and smiled his way. "Hey there."

"You look busy. I'm not interrupting anything, am I?"

She studied him for a long moment. Her gaze went down him and then back up in slow assessment. "Nah. Come on in. What are you up to?"

"Just enjoying the afternoon."

"By being inside?"

He lifted a shoulder. "I guess so, because I'm enjoying myself right now." He came around the corner and peeked in the assorted bowls. White powder filled most. Chocolate chips and nuts were in others. "What are we making?"

"Cupcakes and maybe a few other things. I need to test the heat of the ovens."

Looked like a lot of things just to test the ovens. Not that he knew exactly what testing the heat meant. "I don't mind sticking around to taste the results."

She picked up a fork and spun eggs into yellow foam. "Not hiding from your neighbor again, are you?"

"Maybe a little bit." He pointed at all the bowls. "All that for a few cupcakes?"

She cleared her throat. "I may also be doing a little hiding myself."

He eased on the stool around the corner so not to crowd her as she worked. "You've been back like two days. How are you already hiding from somebody?"

She blew a breath at her bangs. The hair lifted up and then flopped back down where they were. "Grandma and her endless guilt trips."

"Jane's wedding cake?"

"Yep. Grandpa told me Jane already has a cake ordered from Sam's Grocery, but Grandma is determined to change my mind."

"That sucks. No uneven cake on a tinfoil board."

She laughed. "Unfortunately not."

He took another glance around the room and all the pans. Granted, he didn't know a whole lot about baking or cooking in general, but he gathered it had taken her a while to bake the amount of stuff spread out around the room. "How long have you been hiding out here?"

"Umm." She dropped the eggs in some white stuff under a mixer. She hit the button and it hummed alive. "Most of yesterday and today. I've had some things I needed to do. Get my order in. Then my delivery truck came today and I had to sort and put away all that. I also premeasured everything I needed to bake the cupcakes on Thursday."

And today was only Tuesday. "What's on the schedule for tomorrow?"

She winced. "More of this, I guess. There's not too much for me to do until Thursday."

He leaned on the counter. She had a whole free day? Plans were connecting and forming. He could swap days with Jones. Work the Sunday shift—except for during the wedding. Then he'd be working when she'd be leaving, making him off tomorrow. Jones was always up for being off on Sunday, and surely the guy would cover for him for a couple hours. Cade would bribe the man with anything to make this happen. "You could spend the day with me."

She lifted a brow as she glanced his way. "Doing what?"

"Anything you want."

Her fingers were shaking. She grabbed a nearby rag and wrapped them in the cloth. "I don't know."

"We could take off for the day. Ride around on my family's land. That isn't just hiding. That's falling off the map. In some places, there's even limited cell service."

A bit of a grin was starting even as she looked to be fighting it. "You know how to sweet talk a girl, don't you? I can't believe you're still single."

He shrugged. "I know what the ladies like. With the rain we had Friday and Saturday, I bet we can find a good mud hole or two."

She licked her lips and watched her bowl. "I don't know if this is a good idea."

"You said you liked to get off-road. I want to see it."

"Oh, I enjoy it. Maybe a little too much, because that's when I tend to make bad decisions."

"All the more reason to go then. When's the last time you've done something like that?"

"I'm not a complete hermit. I have friends at home and we get out and hit the beach on the weekends."

Girl weekends. "Not the same and you know it or you would have already jumped on the offer."

She licked her lips. "I'm already regretting this."

"Don't waste time on regrets. You're not in town long enough for that."

"Fine, I'll go. But I need to finish baking everything I planned tonight then."

He pushed up from the table. "Where do you want me?"

"Want…you?" She searched him.

"You said you had a lot to do." He waved his hands around. "Put these babies to work. I'm not completely helpless. You remember my oldest sister?"

Her brows pulled in. "Beth?"

He nodded. "She has two short rugrats. We make cookies all the time." From one of those premade dough packages where all you had to do is pull a piece of dough off and put it on the pan. Mostly they ate the dough and didn't tell Beth, but cookies were cookies.

A chuckle escaped her. "All right. Wash up. You know how to use a measuring cup?"

"I'm not completely helpless." He moved to the sink and scrubbed the fronts, backs and between all his fingers. "How much do we have to make to test the heat of the ovens?"

"A few cupcakes, but I like to do a full pan so I know how the ones in the center are going to do. Grandpa never upgraded to convection, so the baking is going to be a bit off from what I'm used to."

He had no idea what most of that meant but found rows of brownies cooling to the side. "What's all this then?"

"I was trying to keep busy. I promised Paula I'd bring her brownies. And then when Grandpa found out I was fooling around here, he asked if I could make a few of his favorite things since he couldn't."

"That's nice."

She nodded and added several bowls of items to the mixer. "Then he went and told his friends and they came back with a list. I didn't have anything to do and was trying to keep busy anyway." She gestured with her elbow to a piece of paper on the wall. "My list is hanging over there."

He scanned over the items. It was a long list of pies, snacks, rolls, brownies and cake. "This is a lot."

She laughed. "Yeah. They're missing snacks since Grandpa has been out of the bakery."

"How much do you have left?"

"I have about three things on the list done. I had finished divided up ingredients for two others when you pulled up." She stuck a spoon in the batter and cleaned it off. With a smile, she dropped the spoon in the sink. "You going to stand there or get busy?"

"Tell me what to do."

She pointed to a row of cookbooks. "Grab that red book up there. It's full of Grandpa's recipes. Look for the chocolate cake. The batter is pretty straightforward and I'll move into the yeast stuff after I finish this."

He found the book and flipped through it. "Is this in any sort of order?"

"Nope. He sticks them in when he gets them. It's there somewhere." She pushed her stool under the table, reached for two other bowls and kicked the mixer up another notch.

By the time he had the page for chocolate cake, she had slid a pan across the counter and spooned cookies out on it. He stepped back and watched her work for a moment.

Her hands were quick and focused as she reached and spooned. Not a drop was spilled or piled out of place. Her attention was one hundred percent on what she was doing and he was struck by how different she seemed doing this.

Without looking up, she hooked a finger on the pan and slid it around to the corner. "The mixer is all yours." She turned, grabbed a tall silver bowl that looked like the one she was currently scooping out of and eased it across the countertop. "This fits the mixer. I found four like it. We'll have to stop and wash after that. I've got eggs out you can use, but since there's two of us, go ahead and grab another tray from the left refrigerator door and another block of butter to warm."

She spooned another scoop of dough and glanced to him. She searched him and as she did, worry pulled on her brows. "Why are you just standing there?"

"I'm moving." He opened the book and found the flour and butter had pounds written next to it. "This doesn't say anything about cups."

She nodded and spun, slid a tray in the oven, swung around the corner and snatched a box of wax sheets as she moved. "Grandpa's recipes are weighted. It's harder for him to see the measuring print on the cups, but he can read the scale display. Use the wax paper for butter. For flour, put the bowl on the scale *first*. It'll balance to zero and then you can add flour."

He grinned. "I took science in high school."

She laughed. "Baking is nothing more than science. Get after it then. All the liquids are still measured in a cup."

She was gone again, off in a hurry doing something else. He found himself standing there once more, watching her move, grabbing this and that. She knew her way around the kitchen, not just in the literal sense, but in every way. Gone was that shy girl who stuck to the walls and tried to blend in. If people could see her in this room, right now while she baked, they likely wouldn't recognize her.

Briefly, he wondered if she would even recognize herself. He got to work on the cake and did his best to stay out of her way. She filled the whole room as she worked with four or five things going at once. Something was always in the oven. Something else was ready to go in. Another pan was greased and waiting.

There was more stuff in a mixer. Bowls were in straight, organized lines going down a table. He'd never seen so much multitasking. Or so many dirty dishes. He cut off the mixer blending the cake and poured the chocolate liquid into the pan she had prepped. He put it with the others waiting on an oven.

No sooner did he back away from his finished cake, did she drop another load of bowls in the sink. Clearly, that's where he could make the most use of his time. He was almost afraid to know what she could do with the added space at the table that he had been taking—plus with the steady flow of clean dishes. He also couldn't wait to see it.

Without waiting to be asked, he started water in the deep sink and plugged the hole.

She came by and dropped another stack of bowls in. "Oh my goodness. Thank you."

"No problem. I think in the time I made one cake, you did ten things. Figure I can be more useful here."

She laughed. "Not quite ten things."

"It's crazy watching you. I don't know how you keep it straight." A little trickle of sweat beaded against her hairline and he resisted the urge to rub it away. Color filled her face. Probably heat from the ovens. Some of it maybe from being flushed with excitement. She'd probably look exactly like that after—he cut his thoughts off right there.

"The bakery I work for is so busy all the time. You can't even imagine what it's like over the holidays. It's like this all day long, with six other people running around you doing the same thing."

"Don't touch what's not yours."

Her eyes widened. "Definitely not. Unless you're asked. You learn to move around each other and generally stay out of each other's way while being in the middle of everything all at once."

"Sounds fun."

She lifted a shoulder and her grin got a little bigger. "Honestly, it really is. There's so much energy. The kitchens there are way bigger than this one. Picture a whole wall of ovens. It's just…it's crazy."

"It's hard to remember you being that girl running with books clutched to her chest compared to you working here."

She grabbed another set of bowls and spread them around the scale. "I ran around with those books so that I could do this."

"It paid off then." He added soap and got to washing the dishes. Most washed easy as the ingredients hadn't been in them long enough to set. Then a couple gave him more struggles and he had to work a little harder.

Just as he pulled the plug on the water, she came by with another stack of bowls and dropped them in the sink. "Good news, I can see the end of the baking."

"Good."

"And then frosting and decorating starts."

He resisted groaning. "I didn't even think about that."

Her smile was as big as he could ever remember it being. "That's the fun part."

The fun part? He wasn't sure she could manage to have more fun while she worked. He enjoyed his job, but this was something totally different. She didn't just enjoy her job. She absolutely *loved* it.

She stood back with her hands fisted on her hips as she took a deep breath and let it out. "Yeah, because of the frosting. There's only one way to get frosting right when you make it."

"How?"

"Tasting it."

"I like that idea." And not because she was practically licking her lips while she talked about frosting. But also because of all the things he could do with frosting and her. He cleared his throat and needed to get his thoughts back on track. If they didn't wrap all this up tonight, he wouldn't have her for a full day tomorrow. "I'm getting hungry."

She nodded. "Me too. And if I don't eat something besides frosting, I'll be sick to my stomach. After I get these last two things in, I vote for a Jasper's run."

"You do owe me."

She nodded. "That I do. And some chicken strips sound amazing."

"After I finish the dishes, I'll run and pick some up." Because if he brought it back here, he could selfishly keep her to himself for a little while longer. Every evening in Jasper's was busy. They'd never have a moment of peace.

"That sounds great. Then I can keep going and maybe get out of here at a decent time." She turned. "Don't take off yet though. I have the final thing for Paula in the oven. Do you mind taking it to her? If I'm with you most of tomorrow and then the next day busy with cupcakes, I won't get to see her while they're still fresh. And she'd love getting them warm."

"Sure."

Off she went again, back in her routine of circling around the table mixing, stirring, pouring, putting stuff in the oven, taking it back out. She took things to the cooling rack and then turned them out on more trays for further cooling.

She pulled out a tan box that he recognized as what her grandpa packaged things in and filled it with banana bread, cookies and brownies. She dropped it by him as he rinsed the last dish and dried his hands. She dusted hers off on a towel hanging from her apron strings. "There you go."

"Chicken strips and do you want some fries?"

She pursed her lips in the cutest way possible. "Cheese fries."

"Now you're speaking my language."

Then she went and stuck her fingers in his front pocket. "That should cover it. And ask Paula to make me a shake."

He had no idea what she'd said. There were words that were probably supposed to make a sentence to convey some thought. The only thought he had was that Annie-Lyn had her hand in his pants.

In his pocket, but still. That counted as in his pants. Annie's hand. In his pants. He cleared his throat and nodded, not sure he could force words to come out, even if he could get a sense of what he was supposed to stay.

At some point, he arrived at the diner. Annie's hand. In his pants. As he walked to the counter and faced Paula, he cleared his throat. He was an adult. He could stop acting and thinking like a fifteen-year-old. Probably. He put their order in, remembering her string of words about a milkshake and asked for two.

He stepped back and a voice cut through his distracted thoughts. The sound caused his throat to close and other vital parts of him to shrivel up and die.

"Cade. I didn't expect to see you here."

He turned and forced a smile for not only his neighbor, but also her sister Jane. "Just picking up some supper."

"Why don't you join us? We have plenty of space."

Thank God, he'd decided to bring supper back instead of bringing Annie here. The night would have been ruined. "I'm meeting someone."

"There's room for two." Tina tipped her head to the side. "And thanks for sending Peter to help me. That was so thoughtful."

"Sure."

She gestured with her thumb over her shoulder. "Let me grab two extra chairs to pull up to the table."

"Thanks, but I'm not staying. I have our order in to go." He wanted to come out with it and say he was taking it back to Annie. Annie was doing her best to avoid almost all parts of her family though, so he'd rather not get into it. "Thanks for the offer."

"I don't mind. Call whoever you're meeting and tell them to come here." She patted his stomach. "It's not good on your belly to eat on the run."

He shifted his feet, easing back a step to be out of touching range. "We've already got plans."

"Are you sure?" She blinked up at him.

"Positive." Like he'd said about a hundred times now.

Tina's smile looked a little frozen as she blinked at him more. Was she trying some genie-in-a-bottle move to make things happen with magic? "Sure. Maybe next time."

He started to turn back to the counter to keep a watch out for his order, but Jane got his attention. She rubbed at the side of her neck. "Peter said you saw Annie the other day?"

"I did." Peter probably thought from picking her up at the airport. Or maybe when he brought her to Jasper's before. He couldn't remember who had been in the diner that afternoon, but if even one person who knew Annie had recognized them, it had no doubt gotten back to Peter or…everyone. He'd seen Annie more than that one time, but he wasn't going to mention specifics because he wasn't interested in talking about Annie without her here. Especially since she had a huge wall up when it came to her sisters.

Jane sidestepped a bit. "How is she?"

"I'm sure she's fine," Tina added and then flicked hair off her shoulder.

Cade bit back what he wanted to say to that, but they were in the middle of the diner and he didn't want to make a scene. "She's really well. Happy. Loves what she's doing, where she lives and is enjoying being home for a bit to see her grandparents."

"That's good." Jane cleared her throat and took another step back. "When you see her again, can you tell her I said hi?"

He blinked. She could have knocked him over. Before he could respond, Tina did. "Why would he see her again?"

So apparently Tina didn't know he'd taken Annie to Jasper's on Sunday afternoon. The rumor mills were running slow. Or Tina didn't believe what was being said or she'd invented some delusions in her head. Anything was possible. Jane lifted a shoulder as she caught his gaze. She glanced to Tina and then back to him. "Well, if you do."

"Sure," he replied simply as Paula called his name in the nick of time. He collected his order and headed back to the bakery where there was no awkwardness, no subtle hints or whatever about anything.

It was just, real. He sat back in his seat for a moment and stared at the old brick building. That's exactly what Annie was. She had this realness. She didn't play the political game in town that created cliques he didn't understand. She was who she was. Take it or leave her the hell alone. She didn't ask for anything of anyone, she simply existed as she wanted, doing what drove her.

He collected their items and got inside the bakery door just as she shrieked. He went on high alert and scanned the room as the mixer that had been running shut down. Snake? Spider? Rat? He saw none of them.

Sweet sugar filled the air and she looked up from a mixer and he realized what had made her yelp.

White was splattered over her creased brows and the rest of her face. "I wasn't thinking and lifted the batters while they were running."

"You must have been in some serious thought."

Her cheeks immediately reddened and his body temperature went up about a thousand degrees. What exactly had she been thinking about? He put the stuff down on a side table by the door and took a second to catch his breath. "I hope it's not ruined." He gestured toward the pot. "Whatever you're mixing. Or were mixing."

"No. It's only frosting. It was almost ready."

He walked over and studied her. Flecks were also in her hair. A big spot was slapped across her cheek. A tasty frosting-coated treat. One he couldn't resist. He swiped off a clump with his finger and stuck it in his mouth. "I think it's great."

Her chin lifted. "Untrained tongue."

Had her voice dropped a little? "I just know what I like."

She bit her lower lip. Her teeth sank into the pink skin and she let it slide free. She clicked something on the mixer, hit another button and it spun back to life. "Don't go anywhere."

"I'm not." He picked another smudge of frosting off her neck. As his finger went over her skin, a swallow moved down her throat. He licked the fluffy cream and sweetness filled his mouth.

Standing over her like this, he had a lot more sweetness he wanted to get his mouth on and have a taste of. She cut the machine off and presented him with a blob of white on the tip of her finger. He held her hand, brought the digit to his mouth and cleaned the soft sugar off. Vanilla covered his tongue and he couldn't say it was overly different than what he took off her face or neck.

He wasn't going to argue though. In fact, he didn't have anything he wanted to say. He turned her hand and licked a spot off the inside of her wrist. The gasp that came out of her was nearly his undoing. It was certainly all he needed to hear to lean in and catch her mouth against his.

Not like last time. Not a sweet, barely there kiss. He pulled her against him and she eagerly met his kiss back. No hesitating like before. She grabbed his shirt and held him tight to her. A breath filled her, pressing her more against him, and he couldn't get close enough as she parted her lips and he got a real taste. The sugariness of frosting filled him in the sweetest way, but her body against him was completely heavy and needy. Warmth filled down the front of him where they touched. Heat flooded his veins and all the sparking energy going off within him made a direct line for his pants.

He was kissing Annie-Lyn. Not just kissing. A little moan purred from the back of her throat and she wadded her fingers in his shirt as the seconds stretched out to a minute—maybe even two of them. This was making out. He was making out with Annie-Lyn. If by some miracle he could play this cool instead of acting like the doofus he was feeling, all his dreams would be coming true.

They just never needed to stop kissing. Ever. He could live in this moment, with her against him, holding him—grabbing at him, really—forever. The double tap of a car going over the railroad tracks outside sounded like a knock and she gasped and pulled away, cutting the best moment of his life way too short.

She cleared her throat. "We should, um…"

He eased his hand around her ear and cupped the back of her head. Her eyes looked drowsy and completely fall-into-able. "Get back to what we were doing?"

"Yes." She breathed out and then her eyes widened. "I mean…no, not that. We should bake." She cleared her throat and eased back a step. "Eat. Eating is what we should do."

"If you're sure." His hands fell away from her as she moved farther back.

She nodded and pushed a few loose hairs away. "Yes. I'm sure."

So not at all what he wanted. He rested on the counter in the middle of the room, trying to soak up all the coolness from the stainless-steel top. "I don't mind if you want to do something else."

Her wide-eyed gaze lifted to his. She held his gaze for a moment and then shook her head. "Trouble with a capital T, Cade Revlin. How did you ever get a job in law enforcement?"

"People say I have a trustworthy face." At that, his phone rang, and he wasn't overly thrilled to see the station as the number. With a heavy sigh, he pulled away from her. "Revlin."

"Neiumer's hearing four-wheelers out behind his house."

Damn it. He pinched the bridge of his nose. This wasn't happening. "It's Tuesday. Who would be out there?"

"I don't know. He wants someone to look around."

"All right. I'll be over there in a few minutes." He clicked his phone shut and looked to Annie as she unpacked food. So close to getting the evening with her. He was the only one on their small town force who had a vehicle to get into hairy places. He'd been the one to dumbly volunteer himself for this type of call any time it happened. "I've got to call this evening short."

Her gaze searched him. "Everything okay?"

He nodded. It was all fine for now. Whoever was out there better hope he didn't catch them. Escorting them off with a slap on the wrist wasn't on his mind. "Some kids are out riding around. I have to go check it out."

She frowned. "It's a school night."

"I know. It's still a little early. Probably taking advantage before the time changes."

"Oh." She looked at the food and then to him. "Do you want me to keep this warm for you?"

As in did she want him to come back? Hope foolishly filled his chest, even though he knew better. The odds of getting back at a decent time were slim to none. "More than likely, I'll be out late. If I catch them, I'll have to hold them and call their parents to come collect them all." Or cart all their asses off to jail and have their trucks and four-wheelers towed. "If I don't catch them, I'll have to talk to Neiumer, who is going to insist I didn't look hard enough and go back out with me."

Her smile was easy, finding humor in his situation. He could too, a little. Some things were never going to change. "We still on for tomorrow?"

"Sure. If you're not going to be out too late."

He could be out all night and he'd still be here first thing in the morning. "I'll be ready to go. About nine? That'll give the sun a little time to get up."

"I'll be here early. Pick me up whenever you're ready."

Now he just had to try not to camp in the parking lot to be here as soon as she got here.

Chapter Seven

Annie filled another bag of frosting, twisted it off and stuck it in the refrigerator. She pulled another one down and that got her a little closer to baking those cupcakes. She grabbed another bag, got the tip on and sat at her stool to fill this one like the four others she'd already put in the refrigerator. After this one, her morning of work would be wrapped up with barely an hour to spare before Cade was supposed to be here.

To take her on a date. Of sorts. Something she probably should have been firm about refusing but she hadn't managed to push the words out. Blame it on his eyes. It was impossible to look at them and refuse him at the same time. Then his hands had been on her. And his kiss. Geez, it was a triple-threat combination. It was all so pointless to spend the day together, but when was the last time she'd done something pointless? She'd been so driven and he was so much the opposite of that when it came to her life.

She set the bag in a cup and spooned frosting over. She'd planned to take care of this stuff last night, but after Cade had left, much of her energy had too. She'd frosted what she needed so she could pack up and leave. He'd somehow taken her focus right out the door when he'd left. Annie had lucked out when she'd gotten home. Her grandma had been in the shower so Annie hadn't wasted time in slipping upstairs to her room. She was close to hiding her car in a pile of leaves if that meant getting by her grandma's watchful eye. More than likely, she was going to have all day Saturday and then Sunday morning until her plane left to endure that fun time.

She twisted the last bag down and had it in the refrigerator as someone pulled in the lot. It wasn't Cade's truck. There was no heavy, sweet run of his engine. This was quieter and car-like.

She wiped her hands off as she headed for the window around the front. She could just barely see the tail end of a white truck sticking out as the engine turned off.

That gave her no clue. Before she'd left town, she could have narrowed down the owner of a vehicle by just the back fender, but aside from Cade and her grandparents, she didn't know what anyone drove anymore. She eased back to the kitchen and got behind her mixing bowl as the knob was turned and the door shoved in. Without even trying—or maybe her knees gave out—she sat on the stool.

Tina, of all people, walked in. She flipped keys in her fingers, caught them in her palm and smiled at Annie. "Hey, Annie."

Annie returned the unexpected greeting, but she didn't trust anything friendly with that smile. Not just the smile, but anything about Tina in general. Now more than ever, she was thankful Tina had stood her up at the airport and sent Cade instead. Of course, if they had been at the airport, Tina would have been nothing but delightful since there would have been an audience. Even if that audience had only been of one security guard. "Tina. Hi, I wasn't expecting to see you."

Tina eased on the stool next to the counter, on the opposite side as Annie. "I thought I'd stop by for a quick visit after I dropped the kids off at school. I don't have a lot of time."

Annie didn't want to just sit there staring, so she worked on pulling off her beaters. She wanted it all cleaned and put away before Cade got here, so they could leave right away. "It's good to see you. Is your son feeling better? Pat, right?"

Her eyes widened at the mention of her son's name. Annie couldn't figure out if she was surprised Annie actually knew her nephew's name or that she cared enough to ask about him. There was really no telling what might go through Tina's head at any given point.

Tina rested an arm on the table. "Yes, it was Pat, and he's fine now. Thank you. Has Cade been coming by here?"

A little heat started in Annie's belly at the mention of his name. Of course, being she was working at the counter where he'd kissed her senseless and this was the spot where he'd talked her into spending the day with him, it was inevitable. She cleared her throat. "A couple of times."

"I thought so. He's an uber sweet guy." Tina's voice hitched a bit as she talked and she tossed her head this way and that. Some people talked with their hands. Tina talked with her whole body. Especially with her hair. Flipping it off her shoulder and whatever. "And he can be very nice."

Annie smiled at her sister and started wiping down the mixer. She wasn't sure what this conversation was going to be about and she'd rather Tina come out with it. If Annie knew her sister, there was a reason for this visit, and it wasn't a how-ya-doing sort of thing either. If she had to take a guess, since this conversation had started with the mention of Cade, Annie wasn't going to like the end of it. She'd like to ignore that uncomfortable feeling settling in her stomach. Like to, couldn't quite manage it though. "He is."

"Right." She adjusted again. Swung her hair again. "I wanted to let you know, before it got awkward, that we're dating."

Annie paused with her rag as she was about to scrub some stuck-on, smeared frosting. She glanced to her sister across the table. "You and Cade Revlin are dating?"

Tina sat a little straighter. "You don't sound like you believe me."

Because she didn't. Mainly because they'd kissed twice. The second kiss had been no sweet, quick, friendly thing in any sense of the word. Not to mention he'd flat out told Annie they weren't. He couldn't be dating Tina. Annie cleared her throat, wanting to be done with this conversation and any other even remotely like it. Why would he do that? Was this going for a chance at his old high-school crush? None of it made any sense, and for all she knew, this was just Tina being her normal self.

It served as a kick-in-the-pants reminder that Annie didn't belong in this town and she didn't want to be here either. She needed to get back home.

"Sorry. You took me by surprise is all." Annie forced a smile, hoping it wasn't as tight as it felt. "I understand. I'm not in town long and I'll be leaving soon."

Tina's smile broadened. "After you make Jane a fabulous cake."

Uh-huh. Annie let that go unanswered and took her rising aggression out on her dirty mixer.

"Do you have designs of the cake yet? Grandpa was working on sketches. I'd like to see them. And take a copy to Jane, because she doesn't have them."

"I don't have any."

Her brows knit together. Bracelets jingled at her writs as she put her hand on the table with a straightening of her back to look at Annie. "How do you know Jane will like it if you don't have a sketch to show her?"

Just keep scrubbing and cleaning. "I haven't talked to Jane, but I understood she had someone else to do her cake."

"Sam's Grocery?" Somehow, even though she was sitting, Tina managed to stare down her nose at Annie.

"That's what I was told."

"No." She made a noise that was probably supposed to be a laugh. "You're doing it because Sam's Grocery is not making my sister's cake."

Lovely. A command. That was Tina. Couldn't say she'd missed that in her time away from home. Annie held some solid affection for the bakery, Jasper's and her grandparents. A few other people here and there. The library. If only she could pick up those parts she loved and take them somewhere else. Or take Tina out of Turtle Pine. Annie could survive here with Jane in town. Jane had the decency to not talk to her and give her space. Annie supposed feeling guilty after stabbing her sister in the back would do that. "I haven't talked to Jane. That's what I was told."

"I'll tell her to come see you."

She didn't have to do that. Annie didn't want to get into it with Tina. While Grandma wanted to guilt trip her into making Jane's cake, Tina would likely stand over her shoulder and browbeat her into doing whatever she wanted. Tina was good at manipulating people. Her sister could be frightening when she expected something to happen.

"I'll send her a message after I leave." Tina pushed out of her chair. "That's all. I wanted to see Jane's cake and let you know Cade and I were dating. You can ask anyone in town."

That still didn't make any sense. She should just let Tina go. Part of her wanted to announce she'd made out with Cade in this very room last night. Just to have something to stick to Tina who always got her way. Not that Annie would ever voice that or put serious consideration to it because she wasn't a horrible person. Still…she couldn't resist a little.

"Does he know you're dating?"

And there went Tina's hand on her hip. "Why wouldn't he?"

Annie cleared her throat and prepared to take the brunt of Tina's wrath for this. She hadn't really thought this through. Then again, maybe if Annie told her sister she'd made out with Cade, Tina would leave and never come back. Annie was a victim in this. Not that her sister would ever admit to that either, but still, for the sake of herself, Annie wanted it out there. "He flirts a lot."

Tina set her fist against her side. "He doesn't flirt. He's very nice. Goodness, Annie, in all those books you read, did you not learn the difference?"

"When I asked if y'all were dating, he said no."

Tina's eyes narrowed. "Stay away from my boyfriend. He was doing *me* a favor by picking you up. That wasn't an invitation."

"I didn't know y'all were dating. I'm sorry." The apology came out before she could stop it. Damn habit. She hadn't wanted to let that part out. She wasn't sorry, she hadn't done anything wrong. But if her sisters had taught her anything growing up, it would be that it was always the other woman's fault. They'd drilled that into her and never let her forget it was her mom's fault that Dad left. Her mom's fault that they were unhappy. Everything wrong in Tina and Jane's life could always be traced back to being Annie's mom. And by extension, Annie herself. So yeah, she apologized. She sighed. Like she was supposed to because she'd rather her sister go away before she launched into asking why a double standard existed.

Because while Annie's mom was a man-thieving whore, somehow Jane was different after picking up Peter. And the biggest whore in this whole triangle—their dad—was somehow special too. Annie was up to her neck in special people with special non-smelling poo. Or so they thought. God, she was so ready to get out of this town and get back home.

Tina lifted her purse and was gone in the same flurry of exhausting dramatics as when she'd arrived. As her car left the lot, a heavy weight landed on Annie as she sat on a stool and looked at the mixer still needing to be cleaned so she could turn around and dirty it right back up again. Her plans for the day with Cade just got canceled.

Because she wasn't doing this. Maybe he was seeing Tina. Maybe he wasn't. Maybe they were on a break. Maybe they weren't. Annie couldn't possibly know, but she was leaning hard on Tina being full of it and out to wreak a little more havoc in Annie's life for good time's sake. This town was way too small for Cade to go around trying to see Annie while also dating Tina. That would never go by unnoticed. It hadn't, since her grandpa had known they'd been at Jasper's the day she'd gotten back.

This drama though? This BS was why she'd left Turtle Pine. In all her years in Houston, she hadn't encountered one bit of drama. Nothing. Yet back home for a matter of days and already there was something.

She rounded up milk, butter and sugar and arranged everything she needed back around the mixer. Last to fetch was the cocoa powder. Five more days and she was out of here. She creamed her butter and started adding sugar and cocoa. Her head was staying down until her plane took off.

Dark cream filled up the bowl. The cocoa would still be too bitter and the frosting tasting nothing like sweet buttercream when Cade's unmistakable engine pulled in the drive and her pulse went up a notch like it was being creamed under her mixer. She started to get up and throw the bolt because that would be easier than resisting him to his face, but she didn't.

She knocked more sugar in the mixing bowl as he pushed through the back door. His charming grin was pinned on her and she returned her focus to the bowl for a deep breath.

"What'cha making?"

"Frosting," she said quickly while trying to maintain her position that she wasn't going anywhere today, because getting tangled up in further drama in Turtle Pine wasn't about to happen.

"Did you still have more decorating to do before we leave?" He dropped his keys to the side and pushed his sleeves up. "Anything I can do to help?"

"Nope. I got it. I think I'm going to be a while though."

He studied her for a moment and then glanced around the room. "Okay. We're not in any hurry. We can go after you're finished. Take your time."

Uh-huh. Time she would take. With her frosting. Her racing heart? Eh, that thing had whipped her pulse into a frenzy the moment his truck had landed in the parking lot. She tapped more powdered sugar in her bowl, careful not to get too much and have it all slosh out of the bowl. She moved to grab the milk and noted her shaking her fingers and stopped what she was doing. Nerves because she was about to dump him before their day? Nerves because he was in the room and she wanted to grab his shirt?

She really couldn't say.

If she was going to get rid of him, she needed to get on with it and get back to work. Working with him around wasn't an option. For her peace of mind, she really needed to get rid of him. "I had an interesting talk with my sister this morning."

"Jane? She stopped by?" He started around the counter. She wanted to get up and put space between them, but if she took her hand off the mixer, he might see her trembling. He stopped next to her and leaned a hip against the table. "I saw her when I picked up supper from Jasper's last night and I forgot to tell you. We got a little sidetracked when I got back."

She would not get distracted and flushed with heat thinking about yesterday. No flushing with ooey-gooey warmth she'd been experiencing since yesterday. Oh no.

She sighed as the temperature in the room seemed to climb a couple degrees. Too late.

"Anyway." He cleared his throat. "She wanted me to tell you hi."

Annie blinked and looked at him, putting the whole issue of him and Tina on the backburner for a second. "Jane said that?"

"Yeah. She asked how you were doing." He eased a little closer and his eyes were so dreamy.

She stood and stepped away as he reached his hand to her lower back. His lips were coming close to touching her temple. And the problem he caused came off the backburner and was put back on high on the front of the stove. No, no. No touching. She couldn't kick him out and refuse the fun day if there was touching. "Please don't."

Those oh-so-dreamy eyes of his searched hers as they filled with confusion. He pulled his hand back and brows dipped. "Is something wrong?"

She cleared her throat and, man, something thick was lodge in there and wasn't letting her swallow. Time to Band-Aid this thing. "I'm trying to break up with you or stop whatever it is we're doing."

"What?"

She turned off the mixer to get some space between them. There was a rag on the corner of the table and she grabbed that to occupy her hands. "Tina stopped by. Not Jane. Tina."

"What does that have to do with us and our plans for today?"

"Everything." She turned around the room, found her stool and plopped down on it. She rubbed at her forehead. This was all such a mess. She could run from this place all she wanted and enjoy her life elsewhere, but that didn't really change anything, did it? She'd come back and it was the same. She wanted to run again. She wanted no part of any of this, and by golly, getting out of here was what she was going to do. "I came here to do a job and that's it. I am counting the days until I go back home. I left to get away from Tina and Jane and all their drama. I don't want to spend the time that I am here dealing with Tina marching up to me and asking me to stay away from her boyfriend."

"*What?*" His eyes widened and mouth gaped.

"If you feel I was leading you on or whatever, I'm sorry. I just got wrapped up." She put her hand down. Why the hell was she apologizing? He'd come on to her. She hadn't sought him out. She was done apologizing for things she hadn't done. Next time she saw her sister, she was going to tell her that.

Ohhh. She fisted her hands. The more she thought about Tina dropping by and staking ownership, the more it crawled all over her and burrowed under her skin. Annie had never been so ticked off.

"Tina and I are not dating," Cade said plainly, directly, and with a tick at his temple. He crossed his arms over his chest. "We've never dated. We're never going to start dating. I already told you that once."

She eyed him. "Look, this is not about me thinking you're a couple. It's not. This is Tina and what my life is with her in it, and this morning was a good reminder." He continued to stare at her and she wanted him to know the full score so he would know exactly what a manipulative… person he had on his tail. "Just so you know though, she made it very clear that you two are a couple."

"No." He closed his eyes and looked down with a shake of his head. "No." His quick gaze could have nailed her to the wall. "Don't cut me out yet. It's not just you."

"What's not just me?"

"Tina is like that with everybody. She didn't single you out. Well, maybe when y'all were in high school she did, but she's very… ah, aggressive. Her coming here and talking to you wasn't behavior she reserves just for you." He raked a hand through his hair. "You remember the neighbor I mentioned?"

She frowned. "The crazy one you hide from?"

He nodded. "That would be your sister. Tina is my neighbor. I avoid my house because of her." He sighed, pulled a stool near and sat on it. His knees straddled hers. He cupped his hands around hers wadding up that dishrag. "And Jane, she's nearly as bad. As soon as I put an end to rumors that we're dating, they come back. I can't get rid of them."

More than anything, she wanted to pull away from his touch, put an end to this right now and escape, but as much as she wanted to do all that, she wanted to stay too. Actually, she wanted to lean closer. "I don't understand. Just tell her no."

He lifted a shoulder. "I've tried. Last spring, Mom had an auction to raise money for the animal shelter. Tina bought me for the day for a honey-do list. Ever since then, she's there. She asks me to go places or asks to do things for me. I say no. I go to Jasper's. She sits at my table. I go home. She catches me outside to talk." He rubbed his head. "When the football games start, I'm already picturing her being glued to my side. No matter how much I step away, she keeps closing that distance. She doesn't come out directly. She…"

"Manipulates," Annie answered. Yep, all this sounded like her dear older sister.

"Yes." Cade looked to her, studying her. "Exactly that. I keep thinking she'll eventually stop. It seems to go on and on. I don't know what's gotten into her or what made her…target me. She goes far enough with the flirting, or whatever the hell she wants to call it, but not so far that there's an actual advance made on me to tell her no. I'm sorry she dragged you in the middle of this. I would have told you, but I know you don't like your sisters. You're only here a short time and I didn't want to waste that time talking about Tina."

"Look." She rested a hand on the table. "You are right in that I'm not staying in town. I don't want to cause any more trouble or have Tina pop back in. I don't know what's going on with her."

"She's delusional. That's what's going on." His tone had lifted and words were coming faster with agitation.

A laugh started, but she stopped it. "I won't disagree with you there, but I'm leaving as soon as these cupcakes are done. This—" she gestured between them, and, God, why was this hurting? She felt bad. They didn't have enough of a thing together for this to hurt, "—this was never going anywhere."

"I know it isn't going anywhere. And for you, I'm probably just some annoying distraction."

"No. Not annoying. Distracting—" she nodded, "—you are that. Not a bad distraction. You're a tempting one."

His brow lifted. "How so?"

She rubbed off flakes of powdered sugar and did her best not to look at him. Looking at him made her want things. Made her want to take her words back for starters. Made her wish she could go back in time and meet him at the door as soon as he drove up so they could start their day together as planned. "You make me think about things that are never going to happen."

"What kind of things?"

"Like living here again." She returned to her frosting to keep her hands busy. "I miss home. I like living in Houston. I like my job and I like the people in it. But I miss my grandparents." She gestured at the room. "I miss this room. I miss parts of town. I miss Paula."

"Are you saying you want to move back home?"

She wasn't sure either one of them was breathing. Then she let out a long, heavy breath that left her deflated. "I'm saying I wish it was an option that I could consider, but it's not. I can't live every day knowing my sisters are right there on top of me. You have no idea how miserable they made me. How it got worse as I got older."

"Is that why you started studying so hard after you and Peter broke up? So you could escape them?"

"So I could escape everything." She shook her head. "Jane left me alone after she started dating Peter. I suppose she felt guilty."

"If they were hard on you, they should feel guilty."

She hadn't talked about this with anyone. The only person who knew even a little was Jane. She rubbed her arms. "When I was fifteen, I thought I was pregnant and Jane walked in on me in the bathroom. I had been crying and was upset. We weren't super close like when we were kids by then, but we had some on and off times."

His mouth dropped open.

"I wasn't pregnant. Just late." She caught him by the arm. Not that he was going anywhere, but perhaps she wanted something to hold on to more than worrying he was going somewhere. "When we were younger, Jane and I could be friends sometimes. Sometimes, I got to pretend we were like real sisters."

"That's horrible."

She lifted a shoulder. It's what it was. "I've thought about it a lot. I was so young when Tina and Jane came to live with us after their mom died. I didn't completely understand why they were there. Jane's my age. She'd lost her mom. She likely didn't understand a lot either. But Tina knew. She started in on me first."

"With what?"

"The blame game." She let his arm go and got back to work. "It's always the woman's fault, you know? Dad slept around, I came out of that. Dad and their mom got in a fight and their mom left during the middle of one. Two blocks over, she ran a stoplight, and that was it. Tina knew exactly who I was. I was the daughter of that woman who made her parents fight all the time. Every time she looked at me, she saw the reason why her parents fought—the reason why her mom drove away from her house that day and never came back."

"Annie." He rubbed her lower back and she couldn't deny that the soothing touch was wonderful.

"It was a long time before I figured out why she always treated me like dirt under her shoe. I was a kid. I thought she was sad about her mom dying. I did everything I could to try to cheer her up. About the time I figured that Tina seeing me is what kept her so mad is when Jane started pulling away. Then one day, it was them against me. It was worse when Tina and Jane were together. When they were separate, Tina didn't give me any attention. I was completely ignored. When it was just Jane, we could almost be friends. But when it was all three of us?" She swallowed past the thick knot that had taken up residence in her throat. "I think Tina thrived on making me miserable in front of Jane. I think she knew Jane and I could have been really close."

"So when you thought you were pregnant, Jane was alone."

"And she was great." Stupid tears started and she blinked them back. "She was that sister I needed. She listened. She hugged me. She said everything was going to be okay. Said she would talk to Peter for me. Peter and I had gotten in a fight the day before and had broken up. We'd been doing that a lot at the time. Break up one day. Back together the next. So Jane said she was going to talk to him that Sunday. They were friends. My life was falling apart, but with Jane there, I thought everything was going to be okay. Do you remember Jenna Laken?"

"Yeah."

"Monday morning at school, before the bell even rang, Jenna ran up to me and launched into this huge gossip story and wanted to know what I thought about Jane and Peter dating."

"God. I'm so sorry, Annie. That's how you found out?"

The best she could manage was a nod. Years had passed and that betrayal shouldn't hurt, but damn it, it did. Not because Peter had moved on so fast, but because despite of all the things Tina had ever done to her, nothing compared to Jane's backstabbing. "Jenna filled me in on the details of the two of them being spotted together Sunday afternoon making out in the parking lot at Jasper's. A few hours after Jane had assured me, that's what she went and did." She shook her head. "I just wanted to be left alone to disappear. So I did my best to study hard. I wanted to leave town as soon as possible and we'd had a career thing at school recently. College was my ticket out."

"You failed. With the disappearing attempt. I saw you all the time."

She pulled her stool up to the counter. "I didn't know anybody noticed me in high school."

"I actually tried talking to you once." He looked down and then at her. "I don't think you heard me. You didn't make it easy. Ever since Jane and Peter got together, you didn't look up at people. You constantly read. You didn't go out. People didn't talk to you because you wouldn't let us."

"I just thought nobody cared."

"Not true." He tipped his head toward the door. "Let's get out of here. Go spend the day like we planned and let you enjoy being home without being anywhere near any of the people who made you hate it here so much."

She bit her lip. Ack, but he was so tempting. She held her ground. "I shouldn't."

"Not too afraid to get muddy, are you?"

She gave him a look. "I don't make the best choices when I do stuff like that."

"All the more reason to go."

She laughed then. The last time she'd gotten in a truck to go mud riding, she'd declared her love to Peter and he'd returned it. An hour later, she'd said goodbye to her virginity and was soon saying hello to her pregnancy scare.

"I thought you weren't a priss?"

"I'm not." She frowned.

"You're acting like one."

"Why does everyone try to dare me into doing stuff?"

"Because it usually works on most people?" There was that smile.

And it was teaming up with his eyes.

"What about Tina?" Yeah, Tina. Who she really didn't care about. Why was she changing her plans and resisting doing something she really wanted because Tina had walked back in her life? She didn't owe her sister anything. According to Cade, he couldn't get rid of her, so it wasn't like Annie was moving in on what Tina actually had a chance of ever getting. She didn't want to be like her sisters in any way.

"I'll worry about Tina." He cupped her shoulders and gave her a little massage. "I'll go to Jasper's right now and confirm with Paula again that we're not together."

"I see I'm not the only one who's good friends with Paula."

"Course not." His grin kicked up on one side of his mouth into a boyish smirk. "Knowing you were close to her sure explains a lot though."

"How's that?"

"After you left, she heard me asking around about you. She's been giving me extra chocolate in my milkshakes ever since."

She laughed. "Sounds like Paula."

"Come on. I'll help you put this stuff up."

"It's really not a good idea."

"I think it's the best thing you could possibly do. Think about it."

"I am thinking about it." That was the problem. She was thinking about it a lot. And she was tempted. Really, really tempted.

"Uh-huh. You look at Turtle Pine and you just think it's a miserable place to be. Deep in your heart, you know it's more. Go with me today. Have something great to remember us by."

"If you think you'll convince me to move back here, stop that dream before it gets off. It will never happen."

"I'm not. I don't want to think about anything today besides having a good time. Let's go get lost on my parent's land. That's all I'm asking for."

She eyed him a moment longer and let out a breath. As bad as an idea that she knew this was, she couldn't say no. "All right."

Chapter Eight

If her laugh got anymore intoxicating, Cade wouldn't be able to walk a straight line, or drive one, as the case may be since they were in his truck. "Told you this was a good idea."

She had her hand on the handle over the door. Mud was splattered across her cheeks. Where there wasn't a splatter of dark brown, she was sun kissed with the afternoon fall light. Her smile was broad and laughter filled her eyes. "Fine. You were right."

He turned the truck down a narrow trail. With the branches hanging toward the center, she buried her face against his arm to duck them. Forget the mud. He could do this all day long so long as she kept her face against his arm with her nails digging into him. But like the other few trails they went down, this one ended too.

And faced them to a wide, flooded area of back pasture. In the summer, his family leased this for hay. After what he was about to do, he'd be out here with the tiller come spring to clean up his mess, but it was going to be so worth it. "Are you ready?"

Her eyes were wide. "How deep is that?"

He lifted a shoulder. "About ankle deep or so."

"I'm ready."

He hit the gas, shifted gears, and his Jeep lunged forward. Water splashed and flew up and crashed down on top of them. Her shriek was lost in the wind with the roar of his engine as he spun donut after donut. So much water exploded around them, he could hardly see a thing. He jerked the wheel around for another hairpin turn and came to stop.

"Oh my God!" She laughed after finishing the words and looked at him. Her mouth hung open. Muddy water dripped from her chin. "That is cold."

"You want more then?"

She narrowed her eyes. "You bet."

He couldn't resist her request as the very cold water soaked his jeans and wet the denim up between his thighs. He did a series of more and more donuts with her cheerful shrieks edging him to go faster, sling the water harder. He thoroughly tore up the hay pasture and brought them back to a stop again. Using both hands, she pushed hair away from her face.

A strand clung to her cheek and he pushed it back for her. "Well?"

She looked around. "I forgot how fun this could be."

"See?"

"Yeah, yeah. You were right. Again. Are you going to make me say it all day long?"

"Maybe."

She'd turned in the seat and faced him. She tucked that foot under her bottom as she often did so she could face him more. He liked it when she did that. It was like she wanted to give him her entire focus. More than anything, he hated his bucket seats for keeping him from pulling her against his side.

He eased his foot off the gas and headed them back out, which would—luckily for him—take them back down that narrow trail. She turned her face in again. This time, instead of grabbing his arm, her hand landed halfway across his belly. He might have slowed down a little bit to draw the moment out. The branches clawed down the side of his Jeep like nails on a chalkboard and he still didn't speed up to hurry through the sound. Not with the way her fingers pulled his shirt into her fist with the excruciating sound.

Eventually, he reached the end of the trail and she straightened. She slid that hand sadly away from his belly with an agonizing swipe. But her other hand? It stayed behind. Lazily hung onto his arm. Her knee was just there to the right of his gear shift where his hand naturally rested. One little move and his hand would find a new resting spot.

She was looking around at the tree line as he drove. Absentmindedly—or maybe intentionally?—she stroked her thumb along his arm. He wanted it to be intentional. He wanted her to be aware of how she was lightly touching him and aware of what it was doing to him. That clinging, holding-on-to move. He dared the chance and moved his hand, landing it on her knee and cupping her there.

She started. The muscles in her leg flexed and then relaxed as her gaze met his. His throat was thick. "Are you hungry?"

"Getting there."

"I bet we can nab something to eat out of Mom. She'll be home." He lifted a shoulder. "If not, we can raid her refrigerator."

She bit her lip as she stilled the hand that had been stroking his arm. "I don't know if that's a good idea."

"Nobody will be home besides Mom and Beth's kids. She babysits them."

She still didn't look sure.

"Peter is at work. Jane wouldn't be there either. You can see the house long before we pull up. So if either of them are there, we can back up and leave. They'd never have to know. I know Mom would like to see you. And you should really meet Katie and Kent."

"Katie and Kent? Beth's kids?"

He nodded. "They're four and one."

She smiled. "Fun age."

"You have a wicked sense of fun."

She lightly pushed on him. "I have a feeling you adore them."

He nodded. "You found me out. I do and can't resist it when they want to run the sirens and lights in here."

"You have sirens and lights on this thing?" She rubbed a hand over the door. "Man, you should have told me that ages ago. This could have been the most memorable of all memorable mud-riding trips ever."

He laughed. "If you're up for going to Mom's, you can see the lights there."

She let out a long breath. "As long as we can leave if Peter or anyone else is there."

"Of course. I would never want you to do something that would make you uncomfortable."

He took the trails around to his mom's house, only taking his hand off her knee to switch gears. Then right back to her leg. It was a comfortable position. Being it was a few inches to the right of where he was used to resting his hand, it was surprising how good it felt. Just a slight adjustment over. Unless he was changing gears. He'd never hated a standard engine so much before.

He topped the small hill and held the brakes before popping out behind his mom's house. It was nothing more than a glorified speed bump. Enough to hide Mom's house from the backside of the property. The bump was good enough for them to try to ramp and crash their bikes on. After they got older, the bikes became four-wheelers. They'd mostly landed those jumps.

He paused as he crested over the back of the hill. They were far enough away that he could let off the brake and they'd roll back into the woods if someone was there, but only his mom's blue car was parked by the house. Two little kids were running between swings and he grinned at seeing them there.

He gave Annie a little squeeze. "Looks like it's just Mom."

She nodded. "Okay. I always liked your mom."

Everyone adored his mom. Not that he could blame them. When it came to moms, his broke the mold. In school, he hadn't always thought so. She had a no-nonsense look that would straighten out a convict. She'd put it to use often when they were kids. The look somehow disappeared for his niece and nephew. Even that time they'd made mud pies on her padded outdoor furniture.

He got closer to the house and his niece, Katie, waved both her hands over her head. Little shrieks yelled over the power of his engine. Kent started to run toward him, but Katie caught him by the arm, stopping her younger brother hard enough he fell on his bottom. As he got his truck turned off, the wails started.

Katie faced him, finger pointing out at him as she lectured. "You can't run at cars, Kent!" She gave her little brother his mom's famous stare. Looks like it wasn't retired after all. She shook her finger. "Do you want to get runned over?"

Kent blinked at her and set his mouth in a firm line. The tears ended.

Cade glanced to Annie and found her with a little smile on her face as she stared at the kids. Her head was tipped to the side. She caught his gaze. "Very cute."

"Just don't let Katie hear you call her cute or pretty and especially not a princess."

"No?"

Before he could get anything out, Katie had launched herself into his arms and Kent was dancing at Cade's feet, reaching up with his arms.

Katie's arms went around his neck and she smacked a wet kiss on his cheek. "Uncle Cade!"

Kent's tippy-toe dance grew to include whimpers. If he didn't get him, those whimpers would advance to wails. He reached, caught the boy under his arm and brought him up to his other hip. "What are you two doing today?"

Kent just hugged him and Katie filled him in. "Well, we watched a movie this morning."

"You did? What movie?"

"Peter Pan." She waved her warm, which wiggled her whole body as she pretended to have a sword. "I was Cap't Hook."

He chuckled. "That doesn't surprise me."

He turned, looking for Annie and found she was already there. Her smile had gotten bigger, and it rocked him back on his feet.

Katie squinted at Annie, faced Cade and then looked to his truck and he knew what was coming. He was going to be in trouble. "You went mud riding without me."

He winced. "I'm sorry. Next time."

She eyed him. "Saturday."

"The wedding is this weekend. We can't."

She picked at her nails. "Momma is making me wear a dress. I don't want to go."

He looked at Annie as he hefted Katie up higher. "Katie here is our resident tomboy. No icky dresses for her."

"No way," Katie announced.

Annie smiled. "Can't blame a girl for knowing what she likes."

"Cade." His mom stepped out the backdoor. "I thought I heard you drive up. What are you doing here?"

"Planning to bum some lunch."

"Of course." Her gaze moved to Annie. "Who's that?"

Annie's hands went over her hips as she faced him.

Kent was wiggling and he lowered both kids down. He put a hand to Annie's back. "Mom, do you remember Annie Cookie?"

His mom blinked and looked her up and down as she crossed the yard to them. "Oh my goodness, Annie, look how you've grown up. I heard you were here."

"It's good to see you." Annie didn't know what to do with her hands. If she hugged his mom like she wanted, she'd get her filthy. She clasped them in front of her to resist the urge. "You haven't changed a bit."

His mom had nothing but affection all over her face. "I always liked you." His mom looked between them both. "What are you two up to? I thought you were working today?"

Cade pushed his hands in his pockets. "I swapped with Jones for the day."

"Come on and sit down."

Annie looked around. "I don't want to get the inside of your house filthy. I know my clothes are soaked."

His mom studied them both. "Yeah, you're both pretty nasty. It's nice out. We can sit on the patio. I was just fixing up some sandwiches."

Annie looked at herself and then to his mom. "I would offer to help."

His mom backed away as she chuckled. "That's okay. I'll let you distract the kids instead. I finally sent them outside to get them out from under my feet while I cooked."

Annie nodded. "Two distracted kids, coming up."

Katie was back and grabbing on Cade's arm. She pointed at Annie. "Who's that?"

Cade dropped to a knee. "That's Ms. Annie."

Annie lowered next to him and gave the girl a smile and leaned in for a whisper. "But you can just call me Annie."

"I like that name."

"Thank you." Annie pivoted around on her foot and pointed at Cade's truck. "I heard that your Uncle Cade has some cool stuff on his truck and that you and your brother are the *only ones* who can get him to turn it on for fun."

He grinned at her slight tweaking of the tale. Without a doubt, she'd won his niece over.

Katie continued the whispers. "It's a police car…in disguise."

"Cool." Annie's eyes widened as expected.

Cade rubbed the top of Katie's head. "You know the payment, Katie."

Katie's little head tipped. "Fine."

She walked into him, hugged, and gave him another kiss. "I love you, Uncle Cade. You're my favorite uncle."

He patted her back. "That's my girl. But let me spray it off real quick."

She peered up at him, turning her little chin up and slaying him with big blue eyes. "Can I help?"

He winced. "The water is going to be cold. Can you show Annie your toys and give her the lay of the land instead?"

Katie nodded and stuck her hand out to Annie. "This way."

Annie slipped her hand in his niece's and Cade sat back on his heels to watch the pair go off. He patted Kent on the bottom. "Better go with your sister. If you stay here, you'll be taking a bath."

His nephew's eyes widened at the B word and he ran after his sister. Cade chuckled. He turned the hose on full blast and opened his door to get the seats sprayed out first so they'd be dry by the time they finished lunch.

He walked around to the other side of the vehicle. Spraying from over here, he was able watch as Katie pulled Annie down at her sandbox. Annie wasted no time in kicking off her shoes and sitting on the edge of the sandbox. Her feet went right in the dirt and the two girls giggled at one another.

After another few moments of digging, the three of them had some sandbox toys and were using them for airplanes. Over the sound of the water, he could barely hear their motor noises of the planes landing in the sand and taking off. Annie had one hand chasing down Katie's plane while Kent stood and tackled her arm to the sand.

Annie's stunned, "Hey!" went across the yard. "You shot me down!"

Kent just smiled.

Cade hit the water across the back end as his mom appeared and rounded the front turn. "Sandwiches are done."

"Thanks, Mom. Katie wanted to see the lights, so I was spraying it off so they wouldn't get filthy."

"Thank you." She looked across the yard where Annie was keeping the kids fully entertained. They were out of the sandbox and playing chase. Annie was some sort of slow-motion zombie monster by the way she walked and her arms were out. No doubt Katie's idea. "I've heard you've been chasing after her."

"I wouldn't call it chasing."

His mom glanced at him, efficiently seeing right through him. "Seeing her every day is chasing."

He lifted his shoulder. "Then maybe I am. Is there something wrong with that? I figured you'd be happy seeing me chase a girl."

"Nothing wrong with it. I always liked Annie. Sweet girl."

"I'm hearing a but."

"Jane mentioned she wasn't staying in town long."

He lifted a brow. "Jane talked about her?"

"Not too much. She was more or less talking to Peter in the kitchen. I was listening in."

He winced. That could go either way. "They say anything bad?"

"No. Why?"

"They haven't been close since they were kids. There was a big fight between them."

"Ah." His mom nodded. "That explains that." At his look, she continued. "Peter was telling Jane she should talk to Annie while she was here. Jane looked uncomfortable about the whole thing. I guess because Peter and Annie dated before they got together?" She shrugged. "Seems like nothing to be so worked up over. It's a small town. Friends and sisters are going to date exes."

If only that's all it was. "There's a good bit more to the story than that."

"Well, anyway, I'm not sure Jane plans to say anything. She seemed determined to give Annie space."

He thought back to Jane asking him to tell her hi. Looked like Jane at least felt bad over what had happened. Annie was now running through the yard, chasing the kids. He hated knowing he likely wouldn't ever see that again. Hated knowing that at the end of this week, she was going to disappear on him again. He hated so much about this whole situation. There had to be a way to fix some of it. Knowing Jane was respecting her space might be enough for Annie to want to see her sister, but he was betting probably not. "Don't mention it to Annie. I don't want to make her uncomfortable."

"I won't." She patted his arm. "Lunch is ready whenever you get done. That's what I was coming to tell you."

"Thank you."

"Glad you stopped by. I don't ever mind a break away from the kids. By the time Annie gets done with them and they eat, they'll crash for a nap."

He laughed. Knowing his mom, she probably would too. He'd seen the napping in action. The three of them cuddled on the couch with a movie. All of them with their heads tipped over. Maybe one day kids of his own would join that picture.

He found his gaze straying back across the yard to Annie. But not with her. As much as he wanted it, and no matter how much he liked her, she was bound and determined not to stay in town. Part of him hoped he could like her enough, care for her enough to keep her here.

But that was crazy thinking. She was only here a few more days. Even on the best of terms, he wasn't sure he'd be able to talk her into staying. Especially not with the issues she had between her sisters. What his mom said echoed back through his mind. Unless he could get the two of them together. Maybe if they were locked in a room together and the only way out was to talk. He needed to find Jane.

"Oh boy." His mom chuckled. "You have it bad."

He blinked and looked at her. "Have what?"

She just shook her head. "She's the one, isn't she?"

Annie had always been the one. The one he could never have. The one who'd gotten away. The one who'd come back to give him a second chance. The one who was going to get away again. He sighed. "Doesn't matter. She's leaving in a few days."

"Then you need to change her mind." She patted his arm. "You can do it. Her family is here. Look at her." She gestured across to her pushing the kids on the swings now. "You can tell by looking she loves kids and family. I know she was close to her grandparents growing up. A girl like that doesn't want to stay away."

"It's complicated."

"You have a few days left to uncomplicate it."

He watched Annie with his nieces and nephews a little longer while he finished cleaning his Jeep. Knowing she was leaving was already making his chest tight. He had to talk to Jane.

Chapter Nine

Annie had always liked Penny Revlin. After all the years away from home, it was easy to forget her favorite parts of being here. Meals were one of them. It'd been ages since she'd sat around a table surrounded by people she'd known her whole life. Lots of laughter was washed down with good food. Even though sandwiches were placed on the table, Annie knew they'd be excellent. Penny Revlin didn't just make sandwiches.

She made *sandwiches*.

Toasted sandwiches on sub bread. Potato salad. Lemonade that Annie would guarantee was homemade. A tray of pickles and veggies with dip. Another bowl with grapes. The kids ran to the table as soon as she gave the word.

She handed Annie a bottle of soap. "You and Cade try washing up with the water hose enough to get your hands clean."

Annie happily took the bottle. "Thank you."

Cade had the water aimed at his windshield. He flashed the hose at her as she walked closer. The spray touched the grass just before her feet and she gave him her best look. "Don't even think about that."

"But I already have." His grin was broad and boyish and she wanted to get her arms around him. Especially get her fingers in his hair that was left wild by the wind and water. It might be a mistake tomorrow or when it was time to leave, but thank God, she'd listened to Cade and gotten in that truck with him.

She sighed. "Lunch is ready and your mom said to wash up."

He aimed the hose at the front of his Jeep and lowered it. "That'll do her good enough. Let me wind the hose up a little."

She waited by the spigot as he made a neat circle with the hose until the end with the sprayer was waiting to be dropped on top. They washed and he draped his arm across her shoulders as they walked to the table. Just across her like that always happened.

Guys had put their arms around her, but she'd always felt more resting post and less of a girlfriend. Cade's arm went around her and didn't really hang so much as held. He pulled her in and made all her endorphins wake up and shoot sparks of happy sighs. She put her head against him to see what it would feel like. Amazing. Simply amazing. So much so that she let her head rest right there against him while they walked the too-short length to the table. He rested his hand at her lower back, keeping it all gentlemanly since he was sitting down with his family.

Sandwiches were passed around and his mom used tongs to fill the kids' plates. "I hear you're working in your grandpa's bakery?"

Annie nodded and filled her plate. "Yes, ma'am. I came in to do cupcakes for the school."

Katie perked up and her already big blue eyes widened. "Cupcakes?"

She nodded at the little girl. "That's right."

Cade's arm went back around her in a possessive hold that she was eating up like her favorite cake. "Annie here is the best baker around."

Wide eyes were back on hers. "Better than Mr. Cookie?"

"Mr. Cookie taught me all his secrets."

Katie gasped and was holding her breath. "Do you know how to make no-bake cookies?"

She chuckled. "I sure do."

"Those are my favorite."

"I love those too." She leaned toward the little girl. "The best time to eat them is when they're still warm."

"We always eat Nana's like that. She gives us a spoon," Katie announced.

Penny blushed. "Baking has never been my specialty. My no-bakes never set so we eat them runny."

Annie nodded. "I've had my fair share of runny no-bakes. I kind of think they taste better that way, but I eat way too much since I'm spooning out of a bowl."

Penny chuckled and wrapped Katie in a wiggling, tight hug. "I think that's why this one likes them so much. She eats until she gets a tummy ache."

Katie's gaze went back to Annie. "Can you make us some cookies?"

Annie winced. "I can try. I have a lot of cupcakes to make tomorrow."

Penny finished her sandwich. "When are you taking them?"

"Friday. All seven hundred of them."

There went Katie's eyes. "Seven hundred cupcakes." She looked to her nana. "Have I ever seen that many cupcakes?"

The older woman laughed. "I don't think you have."

"Please," she begged. "Can I see them? And when I do, can I have some no-bakes too?"

"We can try." Annie already knew she'd move anything to get those cookies. She didn't care if she was making cookies at two in the morning, they would get done before she left.

Cade cupped his hand on her shoulder as he drew her in. "I've seen her in action. I bet you anything she can handle it."

Katie eyed him, then her, then back to him. "If she can't do it, you have to take me shooting cans."

Shooting cans? She looked to Cade. He only seemed in deep thought as he stroked his chin and looked at her. "Hmm. Now I know my Katie Bell loves to shoot her some cans for supper. It sounds like you're betting against winning a cookie."

Katie's grin, the cute thing, got even bigger. "It's a win-win, Uncle Cade."

Cade gave her another squeeze. "All right, Annie. Ball's in your court. You get the cookies done, Katie gets to treat her sweet tooth. If you don't, it's cans for supper."

She searched him. He was kidding, right? "Shooting cans?"

His mom chuckled. "It's a harmless little .22 and they have fun." She pointed to a fence off the yard. "They line a bunch of cans along the fence and help Katie get some target practice." Her smile got a little bigger. "He's right there with her and doesn't turn her loose with a gun or anything like that. Cade's dad taught him that way. He used to come in the kitchen with a bag of cans and say it looked like it was canned soup for supper." She laughed more. "And now Cade is teaching Katie."

Just like he would one day teach his own kids. Annie looked across to the little girl waiting to hear something. Annie nodded. "I'll see what I can do, but I'm thinking you can talk your uncle into shooting cans even if I get the cookies done."

"You think so?" Her eyes widened and went between the two of them.

"Oh yeah. I happen to know your uncle has a super soft spot."

"Where?" she whispered in awe.

Annie patted Cade the center of his chest, not realizing the intimacy of the motion until after she'd already done it. She found his gaze hot on hers and she had to remind herself she was around a patio table with his family. She cleared her throat and looked back to Katie. "Right here. If you double up on those hugs and kisses like you give to get the lights on his truck, I know he'll take you."

"Hey, now." He squeezed her again, this time keeping her pulled in. "Don't give away my secrets. I'm defenseless against hugs and kisses. Especially when she throws in that favorite uncle stuff."

Giggles rent the air, and in a flash, the girl was around the table and climbing all over him. Poor Kent, he didn't have a clue what was going on, but he was right in the middle of it.

His mom pushed up from the table. "All right now. You two are supposed to be settling down. Not getting wound up."

"No." Katie pouted. "Not nap time, Nana."

"Yes." his mom grinned. "My favorite time of the day."

Katie looked at Annie and whispered. "Will the hugs and kisses thing work on Nana to get out of naps?"

Annie giggled with her. "Probably not, but it wouldn't hurt for snacks later."

Then all at once, Annie had an arm full of Katie, and then Kent, who had so far watched her more than interact, was also on top of her.

His mom pushed off the table. "All right, you two. It's that time. Say your goodbyes and go find us a movie. Strip your clothes off once you get inside too now that you've wallered all over Cade and Annie."

Kent was first to go. He didn't bother with goodbyes and eagerly ran inside. Penny laughed. "I think someone has a movie in mind."

Katie stood. "That one with the dogs. Can we watch that until he falls asleep and then swap to my robot one?"

"We'll see."

Katie hugged him. "Bye, Uncle Cade."

Then, to Annie's surprise, she turned and hugged her. "Bye, Annie. When are you coming back?"

She bit her lip and withheld that she wouldn't be back. She just couldn't say it. Cade was looking at her over the little girl's head. She couldn't say it for so many reasons. Reasons that weren't strong enough to keep her here though. "I don't know."

"I hope soon." Then she ran off.

Annie stood and helped gather dirty dishes.

Penny stacked the cups and plates together. "What are you two doing for the rest of the day?"

Cade leaned on the table. "I don't know. We might go back to the mud."

Annie looked to him. "You already sprayed off your truck. I'd hate for you to get it dirty again."

"I would offer to take you to my house, but…"

"Tina." She sighed.

"Oh." His mom perked up. "You told her about Tina?"

Annie laughed. "Tina confronted me. Cade clarified."

"Ah. She's a, um, one determined young lady."

Annie laughed again. "That's a pretty polite description."

"You two are welcome to hang around here. Take a nap with us if you like, but you'll have to have showers before getting on my furniture."

Cade nodded. "I guess all my old clothes are still upstairs?"

"Still hanging in the closet where you left them, as far as I know." She picked up the plates. "I better get in there with those kids and get them settled."

He looked to Annie and cocked a brow. "Showers sound good, and I bet I've got something that will fit you."

Oh no. That didn't sound like a good idea. "That's not necessary. I can clean up at home."

"But then I'd have to take you home. And I don't want to drop you off yet. I know if my jeans are stiff from being wet, yours are going to be too."

"They are stiff."

"Come on." He pushed off the table and held his hand out.

She shouldn't, and yet she couldn't turn away either. She slipped her hand in his and let him take her inside. He quickly pulled her through the kitchen that she hadn't seen in a long time and right for the narrow staircase she'd never been up. She'd been young enough that the Revlins hadn't allowed her upstairs to Peter's room.

The walls were covered in photos. From school pictures of all the kids and some of Katie and Kent. Cade pulled her so fast that she only got a glance at them to recognize the people in them.

At the top of the stairs, he took her to the right. His hand tightly held hers and they stopped at a small bathroom. He flicked lights on and let her in ahead of him. "Let me go dig in my old closet and see what I can find."

"Okay," was all she could say. Because she didn't want to say no. That must have been what he wanted, because he was gone, pulling the door closed almost all the way.

She stepped away from it so he wouldn't hit her with it when he came back in. She leaned to the mirror. It was a wonder the kids hadn't screamed in horror when she'd gotten out of the Jeep. By the amount of mud on her face and splattered in her hair, she could see where Katie had gotten the idea to make her play the part of a mud monster earlier. Even with the dirty-water bath in those last turns in the field, the mud remained.

She pushed away from the mirror and turned toward light spilling in from the bathroom window. It looked out over the backyard where Cade's Jeep was parked. Where she'd chased the kids around the yard. Beth's sweet kids.

There was a summer or two in there where her childhood hadn't been too far off from what Katie and Kent were getting. Wonderful days she'd spent running with her grandpa and then later napping in front of a TV. Bugs Bunny and Daffy were always going on with each other about something or other while she dozed and rested for another round of playing before supper.

That had been on the weekends. During the week, she'd often camped in a room at the bakery in front of a TV when she was little. As she'd gotten older, she'd climbed up on a stool and learned to use the mixer. Then Tina and Jane had come along.

Tina was always with her face buried in a diary or on the phone, but for a couple of really great summers, she and Jane had run through sprinklers in their underwear.

The door squeaked and she looked over her shoulder as Cade walked in. His gaze travelled down her and the corner of his lips came up as he took her back in until his gaze was on hers. "I was hoping to get lucky and find you naked in the shower by now."

A small chuckle escaped her. Yeah, okay, that idea wasn't even close to end-of-the-world bad. Looking him over again, his strong arms, tight jeans and that sweet—but naughty—smile of his. Other than the fact that she wasn't staying and this could never go anywhere, Cade joining her in the shower sounded like the best idea she'd ever heard. Except she didn't dare be disrespectful. "Not with your mom here."

He eased a little closer and his hand found her waist. "She's sound asleep. Will be for at least an hour."

All she needed was for Katie to wake up and go exploring. "I don't think so."

He sighed. His hand left her side and he pushed hair off her shoulder. "Can't blame me for trying."

That she couldn't. "Thanks for bringing me here."

His eyes widened. "I'm glad you had fun."

"I did."

He put clothes for her to wear to the side and warmed her arms with his palms. "I wish I could say we can do this again."

She couldn't look at him and dropped her gaze to the white countertop. "I know."

"We can, you know."

She nodded. If she stayed. But she couldn't stay. Turtle Pine wasn't for her. It was miserable and torture. When she'd lived here before, all she'd wanted was out. She'd been like that cartoon character yelling, "Let me out, let me out, let me out!" Now parts of her were stirring and changing. She felt like the other character running for his life, shouting, "Let me in, let me in, let me in!"

Getting in though, would be putting her in a bubble. This fragile bubble that only existed because she kept her head down and stuck to herself. It could be considered cozy for a while. She'd have her grandparents back. Pick up slack in the bakery to let her grandpa have more time off. Then there was Cade and whatever this thing was between them that kept her heart racing and aching for more.

That dream was impossible and was forever going to stay a dream. As well as she'd avoided her sisters so far, this was a small town. She couldn't keep it up forever. Tina was already trying to sliver in. The walls of the bubble would shrink. The fragile, thin wall would turn to a cage with her frantically shaking the bars to please be let out.

Tears pricked at her eyes.

"Hey." He cupped her cheek. Rough palms held her softly. Course fingers stroked her cheek. "What's the matter?"

"Just…" She sighed. "Torn."

He stepped in. That hand stayed on her cheek, but the other went around her back and brought her in close. Put her in that oh-so-tempting bubble and turned her face to his. "What do you want?"

"A perfect world."

"So make it that way."

"I can't," she whispered. She closed her eyes as a tear leaked out and made tracks down her face. "I want to have more days like today where I chase kids around a yard and have lunch afterwards. Then check in with my family later."

"You can have those things."

"I know. But they come with so much baggage."

"Your sisters?"

"Yeah."

"They're just two people in a town of three thousand."

"That's what they were before, and trust me, even though they were only two of them, they were a lot."

He dropped his head to hers. "You should know I've decided to spend the next few days trying to change your mind."

It was stupid, so stupid, and yet she wanted him to. She couldn't fall in love with him. She just couldn't, because it would never work out. Tina would belittle her. Comments muttered anytime they were near that would prick her skin and stab her heart. Jane's mere presence would cripple Annie. The moment the three of them ended up in the same place? Annie didn't even want to think about that. Tina would have Jane back in her corner and Annie would be back to being that girl who felt like the world was against her.

She rested her head on his shoulder. "I wish it was as simple as changing my mind. You'd also need to change Tina and Jane's."

He left a kiss to her forehead. "I'm not giving up on you."

Chapter Ten

Cade rested against the counter in the kitchen and sipped water. What a difference a week could make. Hell, not even a full week. Just a few days ago he hadn't had much going on in his life that got him excited besides work. Now here stood, breath tight in his chest as he waited for the girl of his dreams to come down those stairs. It was going to hurt like hell when she left and broke his heart.

The steps creaked and his heartbeat seemed to stop until her foot appeared and then she was down the stairs within moments. She lifted both hands to her head and pushed wet hair back, delivering a glimpse of one of those many dreams he'd had over the years. "That shower felt great."

So had his, and maybe he should go have another, far colder one. But he wouldn't waste what time they had left. "How about a walk? They should be waking up in half an hour or so. If Katie has to go home before she gets to see the lights on the Jeep after I promised, I'm going to be in trouble."

"A walk would be great."

He got her as far as outside when he stopped and pulled her toward the Jeep instead. "How about a ride?"

"You just cleaned it."

"We won't get dirty again."

She eyed him for a moment and a breath held in his chest. Would she see right through his not-so-innocent request? He was aiming to convince her to stay. Taking her up the mountain a little bit to Heaven's Ridge seemed like a good place to start. Plus, it would be secluded this time of day, and he could get back to where his head had been going when she'd showered.

His oversized shirt and cotton pants hung off her in the most cuddly-looking way possible. He wanted to back his truck up to the ledge, sit on the tailgate with his arms around her shoulders and watch the sun go down. Her lips lightly tipped up and she nodded. One little agreement. She couldn't possibly know the relief stirring in his gut.

She got settled in his truck and, like before, he rested his hand comfortable on her bent knee. This time, there was something new. As he turned out on the pavement, she placed her hand over his. He turned his palm up and caught her fingers.

In part because he wanted to hold on to her as long as he could. And also because he didn't want her pulling away. She'd be gone way too soon and he wanted her as much as he could manage right now.

He turned down the old road that took them around the side of the mountain. The trees were thick, the leaves still green. In another two months, this place would be bursting with color. He wanted to bring her back then. And again come winter to see the snowcapped Appalachian Mountains in the distance.

She eyed the road. "I've never been up here before."

"Never?"

"This is the way to Heaven's Ridge, right?" On his nod, she kept explaining. "By the time people my age were making tracks up here, I was already busy keeping my nose in a book."

He thought Peter would have brought her up here at least once. Knowing that his brother hadn't, Cade was doubly glad he brought Annie here. Since she was an early bird, she'd love it at sunrise. "The best time is at sunset. I wish I had waited to bring you then."

Her quick shake surprised him. "No. I want to see it. I've heard you can see all of Turtle Pine from up here."

"You can." Maybe, if he got really lucky, he could push the time out so they were up there until the sun went down. He winced. Except then he wouldn't get back to his mom's before Beth picked up the kids. Katie had suffered a life's worth of disappointment at the hands of her dad. Cade wouldn't be added on that list, not even over something as small as running the lights on his Jeep.

He turned his truck around and parked it so that the back of his Jeep faced the ridge. More importantly, so the front of his Jeep was on clear display to any kids trying to come up. They'd see his Jeep and turn around leave. Nobody wanted to drive up to make out next to a deputy.

Large boulders lined the ridge. Not naturally. They'd been placed there to keep people from getting too close. He walked her to the edge and the gasp she let out sank through him. He wrapped his arms around her from behind and tucked her curves in right against him. Warmth flowed off her against his skin, and it was starting to be one of those things where he couldn't tell if it was him or her. It was them together. "What do you think?"

"So pretty," she pointed out. "I never realized how small the school is compared to the town."

"Funny when you go back that things you thought were huge really aren't." He didn't just mean the size of the school. He could only hope she realized that too.

"School was such a big part of my life back then. It seemed to take up everything." She tipped her head back. "Do you know why they call it Heaven's Ridge?"

"Because of the fog." He gestured around the edge. "It settles in against the mountain. As the fog starts to lift, sometimes it hangs onto the mountainside while the area over the ground clears. You can see the outer edges of Turtle Pine. It's like you're standing at the edge of a cloud—on a ridge—and looking down on the town."

"Sounds pretty like that."

"It is. I've only seen it once. I caught a handful of kids up here early on a Saturday morning. They'd partied a little hard the night before and passed out. After they left, I came back for a look to pick up trash and saw it. The steeple off First Baptist poked through and the clock tower off the square just behind it." He pointed across to the neighborhood situated on the rise out of the valley. "Slowly, the neighborhood came into view and then eventually the town. It was like someone pulled a blanket off for a big reveal while the sun cracked over the mountains.

The long breath she let out ended with a soft hum. She rested her head against his shoulder and he wanted to do this every day. "Does the tailgate work on your Jeep?"

"Sure does." He pulled her back and they sat side-by-side, feet swinging over the ground.

She leaned on him a little. Not a lot, not even close to settling all her weight against him, but she tipped to the side so that they touched. "I hear you're supposed to be sheriff soon."

His brows lifted. "Where'd you hear that from?"

"Paula."

He rubbed his neck and shrugged as a familiar uncomfortableness settled in his bones. "If my parents have it their way, then, yeah, I guess so."

"Is that what you want? I'm not even sure what differences you'd have in your job. In a big population, I could see it being a lot more work. I don't know about for here though."

"It's definitely more low-key, but the expectations are higher." He knocked the insides of his tennis shoes together. "Not only do I have to be great, but I'll always be compared against Dad. I'd have to be more presentable."

"You said you have that trustworthy face down already."

He chuckled. "That's just part of it."

"Ah, can't forget about the family you'd need."

His brow lifted. "You been talking to Paula or Mom?"

"Paula. But based on what she said, it was summary from your mom."

He breathed out. "Yeah, I don't know. Mom and Dad think my chances of winning would be better if I had a family. It would show me as a family man, so all the decisions I would make would likely be based on that. Without that experience, I may not win enough votes."

"I'm hearing a but. You're not ready for all that?"

"For the job." What could he say? Did he want the job at all? Ever? He hoped he figured out the answer to that question soon. He found the words he'd never voiced before coming out with Annie. "Not really. I've got big shoes to try and fill."

"What I've seen of you so far, I'm sure you'd be fine. Plus, you'd have the support of your dad at your back to guide you along."

He nodded. "I will have that. Even still, Dad won't be retiring anytime soon. He loves being sheriff. I expect my running is at least ten or fifteen years off. The only reason this has been a topic is because my dad is the sheriff and I'm the only one of his kids who's a deputy. And also because I'm not married and I don't seem to have any prospects."

"With the need for a family for a job, I can't believe you're not beating those *prospects* off with a stick."

He chuckled and bumped her with his shoulder. "I didn't mean it like that. Whenever I get married, it won't be for a job. I just won't have the job if that's what it takes." He lifted a shoulder. "I guess that's really my main hesitation with running. Dad had the family to get the job, but the job took him away from the family more than I liked. He always let us know he was proud and stuff, but it would have been nice if he could have been there more."

"Does that mean you're not ready for marriage?" She searched him with her brows pulled in.

He replayed his words and got where she was coming from. "Opposite, actually. I want to get married and have kids. I'm just not going to settle for anyone. It'll either be the right girl or not at all. And if the job means taking me away from my kids, then I want no part of it either."

She looked down. "Paula mentioned you haven't dated much."

Ah, his dating life. Or lack thereof. Could there be any worse topic? "I know what I like and what I don't like. What about you? No boyfriend? Long-term or short?"

"Ah." She breathed out and an airy laugh left her. "I've dated here and there. Most guys don't have the patience to tolerate my drive for work. Sometimes I work weekends. Especially Saturdays once I started doing wedding cakes. It's not like clients can just pick those up the Friday before. I mean, some they can, but the majority—the vast majority—I have to build on site on the morning of the wedding, and they can require additional hours of detail work."

"Sounds like a full schedule."

"That's another appeal to owning my own bakery. Where I'm at, I'm low man on the totem pole and always work weekends."

"Your place, your rules."

"Exactly."

"Do you ever wonder what would have happened if you had never left Turtle Pine?"

A little squint pinched her face. "No. I always dreamed of leaving. It never occurred to me I'd ever want to come back. Even on the way here I was counting down until I could leave again."

"It was that bad, huh?" He couldn't even imagine thinking that. Thinking that he never wanted to see the home he'd grown up in or the people he'd been surrounded by. Their outlook on the same place was so vastly different, it kept spinning his head around.

A long breath slid out of her. "That's my problem. I had coming home worked up to be horrible. The most horrible experience you could imagine. And it's actually been pretty great."

That's the kind of talk he liked to hear. Those words were promising and hopeful and maybe could lead to getting her to change her mind. Still a long shot, he knew, but it felt like there was a chance. He pulled her a little closer to him. "Oh yeah?"

"Yeah. I keep waiting on the shoe to drop. Something to fall out of the sky or someone to rip a rug out from under me. Tina made a pretty good attempt when she stopped by, but even that wasn't the epic terror I'd prepared for."

"Epic terror sounds like a nightmare."

"When it comes to Tina, it can feel that way sometimes."

"That's good though, that it wasn't as bad as you thought." Could that mean that being home wouldn't be as bad as she'd thought either? That maybe, just maybe, she was considering the idea of being home. Actually considering it, not just lightly flirting with the idea of being home with her grandparents like she'd mentioned earlier?

"I think I found her tolerable because of you. Because you were there to explain that she was wrong." She sighed. "Part of what's so difficult with Tina is she always kept herself away from me unless she had a complaint. It's hard for me to tell when she's completely honest or when she's stretching the truth to get to me."

"She knows your soft spot." He rubbed her shoulder. Since Annie wore her heart on her sleeve, he would wager most everyone knew her soft spot. It was no wonder Annie had done her best to disappear completely in hopes everyone would forget about her. It was the only way she could protect her feelings.

Annie nodded. "Yeah. And she narrows in on it like a hawk. I don't want to poke her, and I wouldn't even know where to get her back if I tried." She lifted her arms and dropped them. "She's this complete foreign thing to me. I know she hates me, she always has, and I don't how to fix it or make it up to her. I quit trying."

"Honey." He brought her in and left a kiss on the side of her head. "Sometimes people don't want to be fixed. There's nothing there for you to do. Tina long ago decided to single you out. It's going to be up to her to let you in."

She bumped him with her shoulder. "Thanks."

He wasn't sure whether to mention it or not, but his only hope of convincing her to stay depended on Jane. He didn't want to risk ruining the mood, but if he was going to make a real attempt at swaying her to stay, he needed to know where to start. "If Jane tried to talk to you—have a real conversation—do you think you would want her to?"

She was quiet for a long moment. Finally, she let out a breath filled with so much disappointment, he already knew she was going to break his heart before she got the words out. "I don't think so. It's been so long, I wouldn't even know what to say to her. There's a lot of bad history there that I think should be left alone."

Let sleeping dogs lie. He did his best not to show the heavy weight of disappointment settling on him. Sometimes those dogs needed to be woken up. He did notice though, that unlike the day he'd picked her up from the airport, she sounded more or less sad about Jane. Before, she'd been angry to the point of feeling sick. That had to be some progress. And after only a few days? All good signs. He hoped.

She tucked her legs up. "What time does Beth pick up her kids?"

He twisted his arm down for a check of his watch. "In about thirty minutes or so. We'll have to leave soon." He sighed. "I don't like disappointing Katie. Her dad walked out on her a year or so ago. She's peppy and happy now, but she wasn't always that way."

"Poor girl."

"I know I'm not that guy, but I don't like disappointing her even a little bit. Beth has been through a lot and Katie being difficult didn't help. It was really a huge family effort to turn her around."

She covered his hand. "You're a good uncle."

He sighed and knew how this night was going to end. "Yeah. And because of that, I'm giving up the rest of the evening with you. I won't even be able to keep you here until sunset."

She sat up and left a kiss on the cheek. "But think about all the brownie points you're earning."

She hopped off the tailgate and stretched in front of him. His clothes were big on her. The T-shirt didn't even raise high enough to see her waist or how the drawstring pants might be against her hips. Even with the baggy clothes on, he knew what the sweeping arch of her back would be like as she reached her arms over her head. She faced him and stood between his legs. All his brain functions died. She placed her hands on his thighs and rubbed him there. The heavy swipe of her palms warmed his legs and the rest of him.

She leaned into him. "Few things get to a girl faster than a dedicated family man."

His throat was tight as he fought for words. "Have I told you about the times they have sleepovers with me?"

She laughed and, okay, that worked because she eased closer and the clean scents of soap from her shower surrounded him.

It was a knotted-up mess in his mind. Annie so close he could kiss her, her fingers reaching high enough up his inner thighs that she was nearly touching where he ached the most. Where he was going to have rearrange in a moment if things kept on in this direction. All the hotness of Annie-Lyn at his fingertips and it was the subject of his little niece and nephew that had gotten him here. Throat tighter than ever, he managed a swallow. "It's true. We make forts out of my couches and blankets."

Her lips covered his. "You're going to be a great dad one day."

He wrapped her in his arms. "I just need to win over the right woman."

She didn't pull away from him, but she definitely stilled. Where'd that sexy, open woman go to just now? He'd pushed too much, or had he? He'd already told her he was aiming to change her mind.

Hell, he didn't know what to do anymore, so he went with it. He pulled her in so that the only thing between them was the unfortunate barrier of clothes. She'd just gotten down from the tailgate, but they had fifteen minutes before the absolute last second until he needed to go.

He planned to make the most of those minutes. With that, he pulled her up on the tailgate, over the top of him until he was on his back and she was across him in his arms. Brown hair made a curtain around their face. Her elbows were on either side of his head and every last inch of her stretched across him. She softened on a moan, melting along him like candy in his hands. Her legs straddled one of his and her lower back rested in the perfect spot under his hands. The sweet sway of her back swept out to the curvy shape of her ass. Was a second kiss too soon to reach a little farther and get her in his hands? It seemed like it should be too soon. As her lips meet his in teasing touch after teasing touch, he wasn't sure anymore.

The presses of her mouth became heavier. The full breaths between them forced their chests together so that her breasts mashed to him. She tasted of tart lemonade and he took his tongue across her lips for a better taste. She parted for him, coming out to meet him and to hell with manners and what was and wasn't appropriate. He reached out, got her ass in his hands, and she stiffened for him. Not stopping, but hungry for more. She pressed her hips firmly to his and left him two steps away from begging.

This had become so much more than making out with Annie-Lyn in the back of his truck. Even up here on Heaven's Ridge, where every boy did his best to bring a girl here for this exact purpose. Watching her with the kids today…this was so much more than wanting her to stick around longer.

It was getting harder and harder to not picture her in his life. It was easy to see into next week with her standing in his bathroom, wearing a pair of undies and a tight T-shirt. Nothing else. Would it be morning as she got ready for the bakery or in the evening about two seconds before he tackled her to his bed? Logically, it shouldn't happen this fast. He shouldn't be thinking things like marriage to a woman he'd spent such a short amount of time with. At the end of the day, he'd spent so much time dreaming about her, his dreams were fuzzing over into reality because she was living up to all his expectations. Not just living up to them—exceeding them. She was everything he'd always thought she'd be and with so much more depth and heart that he'd never seen coming.

Every long kiss that went on and on with hardly a break for air, the way she caressed his hair and the press of her body along his all pointed to one thing. And it wasn't just sex. It was this. This intimacy, this clicking that they had together.

He didn't know what else to call it. They clicked. They functioned together and worked in a way he'd never found before. The way her fingers curled against him as the kiss deepened. More than anything, he wanted this to go on and on. He wanted to roll her beneath him, discover exactly how well they clicked together.

The subtle ticking of the second hand on his watch told him it wasn't going to happen. At least not right now. With a heavy heart, he gave her another long kiss. As if reading his mind, she pulled away. Her hair still curtained around them and her smile was brighter than the sunset over Turtle Pine was about to be.

She tucked one side of hair behind her ear. "To be continued?"

He nodded. Absolutely. "To be continued."

Chapter Eleven

Annie slid another tray of cupcakes in the oven. She'd lost count of how many she'd pulled in and out on her fifteenth trip or so. And she wasn't missing that she'd started losing count when her grandparents got here.

To clarify, her grandma. Bless her heart, she was at least washing dishes while she was here, but with the distraction of her nonstop talking, Annie wasn't sure she was making any sort of progress.

It didn't help that last night had ended with her telling Cade, *"To be continued."* To be continued? Who was this girl that said things like that? And who was the girl that was disappointed when he'd dropped her off at the bakery instead of taking her back to his Mom's to see Katie and Kent skipping around the yard while he ran the lights and sirens? The disappointment had nearly been strong enough for her to tell him she'd be fine seeing Peter or Jane—or both—if they'd also been at his mom's house by then. She didn't care. Because she wanted to play with the kids and hang with his mom. She also wanted that *to be continued* to take place after running his lights for the kids.

But in the end, she did care. Because yesterday had been awesome, and she hadn't wanted the end of it tainted by seeing Peter, Jane or Tina. So with a quick kiss, she'd gotten out and done more prep for today.

Her grandma placed another bowl over the dryer rack. "I don't see the problem. You're already going to be here. Why not do this for your sister?"

"Because there's no need to." And she still didn't want to. Tina coming in yesterday had showed her that things hadn't changed all that much, had they? It wasn't a real question. She already knew the answer.

Of course things were the same.

"Annie." Her grandma caught her eye from across the room. "There's only one chance to do this. What if you regret it?"

What if she didn't? What if she caved, baked her ass off and then regretted caving? She couldn't say that. "It's really not feasible anyway. I have hundreds of more cupcakes to bake today. Then I have to decorate and deliver them all tomorrow. The wedding is Sunday and my flight is that morning. Time is a factor here. If I'd planned to do her cake, I would have needed to start Monday."

"That's why I talked to you about this the day you got here."

Only because Annie had brought it up first. Again, she didn't say that. Had she put eight eggs in here or just seven? With a low uttered groan, she recounted yolks. "And I still don't want to do it any more today than I did a week ago."

Except the thought of baking her sister's cake didn't get the skin on the back of her neck to itch like it had before. Probably because she'd firmly settled in the hell-to-the-no-not-baking-it camp.

Grandma's mouth opened, but Grandpa came back through, stopping her. "Leave her alone. I told you a long time ago she wouldn't want to." He looked to Annie. "I counted two hundred and twenty."

She nodded and cracked more eggs. "Good."

"And it's coming up on noon. I think you're doing fine."

"Me too." She'd come in early and gotten to work. She'd anticipated a visit from Cade possibly slowing her down, but so far she hadn't heard from him. For all she knew, he could be across the county busy with something. Instead of planning for a midday break, she'd plan for finishing up early. If Grandma would stop distracting her with questions, she could potentially quit measuring everything twice and pull ahead as planned.

Her grandma rinsed another dish and tapped it off as she placed it in the drying rack. She dried her hands. "That's all your dishes for now."

"Thanks. That was a huge help."

"Happy to, but I'm hungry. Do you think you can take a break so we can run and grab some lunch?"

She poured eggs and sugar together and started the mixer. "I brought something with me. You two go ahead. You've been a huge help and you're supposed to be resting."

Her grandpa frowned. "I didn't call you in to leave this dropped in your lap by yourself."

"I've got it. And I'm ahead, remember? Go enjoy the day and time off." And for her peace of mind, get her grandma out of there. "If I get behind, I promise I'll call."

Her gaze strayed away from him to her grandma, who was over at her grandpa's desk. Darn it, he didn't get her out fast enough. Her grandma lifted a file. "Here's the drawings your grandpa started for Jane. Have you had a look at them yet? Maybe it's simpler than you thought."

Annie turned pleading eyes back on her grandpa and he chuckled. "Let's get out of here for a while. Annie can't stop to look at those drawings right now anyway."

She mouthed a thank you to her grandpa while he ushered her grandma out the door and left her in peace. She wasn't sure how many trays of cupcakes she'd gone through when a vehicle pulled onto the lot.

There was no loud, rumbling engine, so it wasn't Cade. Grandma? Tina? At this point, she wasn't sure which would be worse. And then giggles sounded and she couldn't stop the smile, not that she wanted to.

She filled another tray of cupcakes with batter as the door opened and Katie stood there. "Annie!"

Kent wobbled in behind her, holding his nana's hand. Penny Revlin got him in the door and let him go to shut it. "I hope this isn't a bad time. They've been asking for you since they got to the house this morning."

Okay, there went her heart melting a little. "This is fine. I'm actually ahead. My grandparents were in this morning and got me off to a good start."

Penny set her purse aside. "They wanted to see seven hundred cupcakes."

Annie laughed and led them to the other side of the room, through a door to rows and rows of cooling racks, then into the front room where more were sitting across the counter and the table tops. "Some of them are hot, so don't touch anything."

"Wow," Katie's whispered word filled the room and then she looked a little puzzled. "No frosting?"

"I'll do that next."

Penny herded them back to the kitchen. "Best get back in here before they turn them all over."

Yes. Oh yes. She couldn't start over.

Penny slowed as the kids went on ahead and circled back around the mixers and bowls set around the counter. "Have you heard from Cade today?"

Warmth went through her at the mention of his name. Also, his mom asking if she'd heard from him? She couldn't describe what that felt like. "I haven't, but I know he's working today. I don't know what his schedule is like."

His mom nodded. "There was a really bad wreck on the other side of the county. I don't know any details. Robert called earlier and let me know they'd be over there all day."

"Oh my goodness. Is everyone okay?"

She gave a subtle shake of her head. "Just wanted you to know if you were expecting him anytime soon. Or to see if you'd heard anything. Robert got the call this morning and Cade was already on duty." She pointed at the trays with a clearing of her throat. "How many of those have you baked this morning?"

Subject change. Got it. "I think I'm up around three to four hundred right now."

"I can't even imagine," she said and laughed—though by the tightness around her eyes and the strained laugh, Annie could tell Penny was worried.

Which made Annie worried. Penny should be used to accidents. With her husband being the sheriff and working in law enforcement for as long as Annie could remember, this shouldn't be any sort of new thing happening. So why was she so nervous?

As Katie dragged a stool over and climbed up, Annie pushed the thoughts away to keep the news from the kids. The little girl put her fingertips on the edge of counter and peeked across the surface. "Can I help?"

"I need an official taste tester. Do you think you're up for it?"

Her eyes widened and she nodded so much and so fast, it was a wonder she didn't fall off the stool. "Let me get these in and I'll see what

I can find." She glanced to Penny across the room. "If that's okay?"

"Of course." Relief filled the woman's eyes.

A distraction had clearly been needed. Annie rubbed her hands off. "If there's something you need to take care of in town, I don't mind if they hang out with me here."

Penny bit her lip and looked around. "I won't be but a moment."

Annie rubbed Katie's shoulders. "We'll be good here." She looked down to Kent, whose round head cocked to the side. She opened her arms and he accepted her and she lifted him on a hip. "Did you know my grandpa taught me everything I know right here? I was probably your age."

"Really?" Katie gasped.

Annie nodded. "Yep. You're sitting on my old stool. And you know what?"

Katie looked up at her, waiting. "What," she whispered.

"I was his official taste tester. So it's a good thing you two came in today because I was needing one." Annie glanced across the room as Penny gave her a wide smile.

She shouldered her purse. "Thank you. I won't be long." She put her hand over a large blue diaper bag. "He has toys and everything he needs in here."

"We'll be good." Annie focused back on the kids.

The door closed and left her alone with the two kids, a mixer going around and ovens baking. "First rule of baking is washing hands."

"Awe man." Katie's nose pulled up.

"I know. I hate that part too." She pointed across the room. "There's a stool over there. Can you grab it?"

The girl went off and Annie leaned over with Kent and got his hands washed too. After Katie's were done, they were back around the counter. Kent mostly saw to banging his cup on the counter until he wiggled to wanting down. Annie set him up with some toys in the corner while she and Katie got busy with this batch of cupcakes.

She showed her how full to get the cups and how to rake off the excess. They went through pan after pan until they were making new batter and fluffy, cooked cupcakes were coming out of the oven. She finished up one last batch and Katie was getting restless.

"How about we do some frosting next?"

Light landed back in the girl's eyes as they finished off that batch. Kent was back, bored with his toys as they finished up. With the frosting coming out, the two would be well entertained with eating. At least for a few minutes until the sugar kicked in.

Oh, boy. How had her grandpa ever done this with her always underfoot? She was laughing to herself when she remembered the TV in the back. Of course. She wasn't sure how long Penny was going to be, but Annie would bet that old TV was still back there. More than likely, an old VCR player and some tapes too.

They had all their supplies out for frosting and Katie picked green frosting to start with.

"Can I help?" The little girl was sitting on the counter at the edge. Kent was sitting too, but in the center.

"Sure. I'll have to help you though, because it gets heavy."

She got a plate and started Katie how grandpa started her. On a clean plate so the piped frosting could be picked back up and used again. Annie stood behind her and held most of the weight of the bag. First she demonstrated and then had Katie grab.

"We're going to start on the outside and go round and round. Like

I just did. I'll squeeze and you guide."

Letting Katie think she was doing most the work, Annie guided her around. Frosting cupcakes was more getting into the motion than nailing down the skill. Anyone could frost a cupcake with a swirl if they practiced the circle enough. They did several as Katie giggled and Kent banged his cup on the counter. They filled the plate and started on the first cupcake. They made it all the way through three of them when Katie lowered her hands.

"Is it time to eat one yet?"

"I think so."

Annie fixed their treats up, and while they ate, she piped frosting across cupcakes with a speed that showed the thousands and thousands of cupcakes she'd frosted in the past. She finished off her large bag, swapped out for more cupcakes and did another batch.

"Do you have any sprinkles?" Katie lay on her belly on the counter. Chocolate was smeared on her face in a way that only a kid could manage.

Annie fetched the tray filled with a gazillion bottles. Since the cupcakes were going to the school, she'd let Katie get wild with them. The younger kids would enjoy the sprinkles. They worked as a pair as Kent ended up on his back, still in the center of the counter with his eyes looking heavy and dropping.

They made across all the pans she had on the counter and Annie wiped her hands off. "Let me move him. I think there might be a TV in the back."

"Really?"

The TV was in fact still there, right along with all of Annie's old movies. Katie had one picked out and was cuddled up in the chair with her brother tucked in sleeping next to her. Annie lingered in the doorway a little longer and a little wistfulness threaded through her. And a few unexpected tears pricked the corners of her eyes. She'd be lying if she said she didn't want this. That she didn't want to stand here in this room, baking her heart out with kids underfoot, putting them down to sleep while she kept working.

She wanted that. She'd never realized how much until it was slapped right in front of her. But to move her whole life? Her everything. With a heavy heart, she pushed away from the doorway and went back to frosting cupcakes and boxing them up. That would make less noise than using her mixer to bake the last few dozen she needed. Before doing that though, she grabbed a pot and oats. After a few minutes, she had no-bake cookies cooling on wax paper.

She got them boxed up as a vehicle came back through. Hopefully it was Penny. Not because she needed to pick up the kids, but because Annie wanted to hear news. She wiped off her hands and opened the door to find Penny walking across the lot.

Annie stepped out, leaving her foot in the door to hear if the kids got up, but they were far enough away to talk. "Do you know anything else about the wreck?"

"A tanker truck turned over. I always worry about an explosion when that happens because I know Robert is going to be right in the middle of it." She pushed at her hair. "Now I have to worry about Cade there too."

Now Annie's stomach was in knots. "They have it contained?"

"They're getting it cleaned it up." She sighed. "I'm not supposed to talk about this."

Annie nodded. "I understand."

"But I'm sure Cade will be headed your way, and I think you should know what's coming. This is part of what we deal with when we get in a relationship with these guys. Lots of patience and understanding for the horrors they see."

Annie wanted to correct Penny, say that she wasn't in an official relationship, but then she couldn't manage it either. "I never considered it. We talked before about his job, and I didn't think much beyond speeding tickets. He mentioned breaking up parties."

"That's most of it. Car wrecks happen and they're the worst. This was a family of four passing through. The semi swerved or something. Nobody really knows for sure. It hit the family and wiped them all out." She looked down and breathed out. "Cade was first on the scene. He'll have seen…"

Annie's chest burned. "Whatever was there."

"Yeah." She was silent. "I don't know anything specific. I was told it wasn't pretty. I've heard some horrible things over the years, and sometimes I'm just fine not knowing details."

Annie didn't know what else to do, but Penny was standing right there, so she wrapped an arm around her and brought her in for a hug. "I'm sure they'll be fine and home soon."

She nodded and patted her back. "They will. Robert is already on his way in. He's been back and forth because of the media. He's coming back now so they'll have an update on the spill for the six o'clock news. Cade's replacement is going out in an hour so he'll be here in a little while."

"Come on in. I'm sure Grandpa has some coffee around here somewhere."

Her shoulders softened. "That would be wonderful. Thank you. How were the kids?"

"They couldn't have been better. Kent's asleep and I put him with

Katie for a movie."

She passed Penny a cupcake, set the coffee on and got back to work. She didn't work as fast, not with news of the wreck and Cade sitting on her mind. She did work steadily though. Penny collected the kids at some point and headed home and Annie kept working. She worked up another batch of cupcake batter and whipped out her last few pans until she had enough cake.

Over two hours passed and Cade still wasn't back yet. Maybe he wasn't coming here? She found herself easing away from the kitchen and to the front windows in hopes of seeing his truck. Even though she knew she'd more likely hear it before she saw it.

Her phone was in her pocket and she wasn't going to wait anymore. She hadn't wanted to call while he was at work, but according to Penny, he should be in town and off. She pulled it out and sent a text instead of calling in case he might still be in the department building.

She made it back into the kitchen when he responded, saying he'd be there in a bit. Renewed energy filled her and she got to work on the cupcakes she had out waiting for her. She had most of them done when the sound she'd been waiting for finally arrived.

She paused as she hovered over a cupcake with the tip of her frosting bag and realized exactly what thought had just automatically whipped through her brain without hesitation. Even before Penny had stopped by and told her what had happened, Annie had been on pins and needles waiting to see him. She finished off the last row of cupcakes she had lined out and put the frosting away as his engine cut off.

All that was left was to pop these few into a box. She got as far as pulling a box out when her back door opened. He stepped in wearing his tan uniform and she did a double take. Star over his chest and gun with other assorted things around his hips. His eyes were dark and he looked tired.

Tired and sad. She stopped where she was and crossed the room to him. "Hey there."

He breathed out. "I'd been driving around for half an hour trying to decide if I should come here when I got your text. I don't know that I'll be the best of company."

She wrapped her arms around his waist. The hard padding of his vest was unforgiving against her cheek and made him so much broader that she could barely get her arms around him. "Your mom told me what happened."

She pulled him into the room and guided him to a chair. She started away, but he caught her by the wrist. He didn't say anything, but she moved behind him, wrapped her arms around his shoulders and rested her cheek by his neck. "As soon as I pick up my mess, we can get out of here. If you want."

He nodded. "I'd like that. I'd like to just take you home tonight."

Which would mean being close to Tina since she lived next door. Annie bit at her lip and didn't even care. "Sounds good. Have you had anything to eat?"

"Not since breakfast. I haven't been hungry."

"I'll fix you something. A little food will help you feel better."

"More than anything, all I want right now is to sit in my recliner, have you in my lap, and watch a funny movie to try and forget this day ever happened."

She left a kiss on his cheek. "I like the sound of that."

He rubbed her arm. "Thanks, Annie. For texting. For...everything."

Her heart was hurting as she fell for this man more and more. She was falling so hard and so fast. She cleaned up her mess, shut everything down and went out with him. She left her car and rode with him. He only let go of her to get in the Jeep, and as soon as he was back in, his hand was on hers.

Darkness filled the heavy bags under his eyes. A slump weighed him down. She gave his hand a reassuring squeeze as he pulled into the driveway of his home. A cute white house. Open carport and no patio furniture under the front stoop.

She didn't have to ask which side her sister lived on, since as they pulled in the driveway, Tina stepped out of the house. There was a water jug in her grasp that—judging by her narrowing eyes—was likely in a white knuckle grip.

A little smile lifted his cheek as he faced Annie and pulled the emergency brake. "My tires are going to be slit in the morning."

She laughed. "If my car was in town, those are the tires I'd be worried about. I'm sure this will be all my fault and you'll be the victim here."

His brow lifted. "Seriously?"

"Always."

She glanced back up and found Tina had gone. One confrontation she got to avoid. And maybe since Annie was with Cade, in his vehicle, pulling up at his house, Tina would avoid her the rest of the week.

Or call her a boy-stealing whore. Yay sisters.

She followed Cade through a side door off the carport and found herself in a clean but bare kitchen. No cutesy things on the wall or counters. No rooster or cow or duck theme. Typical oak cabinets, white walls and white countertops. So probably not his most used room in the house. Since Paula had commented at the diner about his frequency in there, Annie feared what food she might actually find.

His hand went across her lower back as he eased by. "I'm going to take a shower."

"I'll join you," was on the tip of her tongue, but she managed to hold that back. Whether he wanted to eat or not, the man needed some food. But that's when he pulled at his button-down shirt and untucked it.

Also the buckle of his belt. Maybe he didn't need dinner. Maybe what he needed was help getting that stuff off. The Velcro of the black vest came apart in a long, slow crunchy-sounding rip. The white shirt under was wrinkled and wet. Probably sweat. He could probably use a full-body rubdown too. By the spark in his eye and turn at the corner of his lips, they were thinking the same thing.

She cleared her throat and looked away. "Okay. I'm going to dig through here and see what I can find."

"All right," was his response and then he was gone. Even long after he was gone, she still struggled to get a full breath. Dinner wasn't going to cook without her and she searched through the cabinets, refrigerator, and freezer and ended up setting the table with chips and sandwiches.

While his deputy uniform was distracting, him walking back through the kitchen in low-slung running pants with a tight white shirt was something else. Both outfits were about the best things ever, in very different ways. She wasn't much of a foot person, but watching him move around the kitchen on bare feet was the most appealing part. He was just so at home. So relaxed.

Everything about her being in Turtle Pine wasn't normal. But seeing him in his house, it was like she was getting a peek into the life of Cade Revlin. He grabbed a cup, filled it with water and then sat in the chair to the right, by the wall and facing the door to his carport as he probably did every day. If she was here more, would this become her pattern? Setting the table while he washed up? Following behind him and sitting at the chair at his elbow?

There would be more to her existence than meal times. Obviously, she would work. Probably in the bakery with her grandpa. Or, according to her grandma, more likely work alone there. After a long day of work, they'd settle in like this. Or around a table at Jaspers like they had before. The thoughts didn't fill her with an urge to pack her bags and get out of town with terror licking at her heels like she'd always imagined.

What was that supposed to mean? That after a few days she was supposed to uproot her whole life and return to the place she'd spent years running from? Doubtful. That wasn't even logical.

Tension was thick in the air as they ate. So thick she wasn't getting anywhere with her sandwich, so she pulled the bowl of fruit closer. He must have decided he was hungry after all since he devoured the sandwich, the chips and was now tearing into the bowl of fruit. She passed hers across to him and he ate that as well. Her heart ached for the sight he must have seen today.

She wouldn't even know how to process that or function. She knew without a doubt he would have been on top of his game for the entire time he was out there. He'd hoped for her comfort to ease the stress that had been laid on his shoulders. What about months from now, when something like this happened again? Who would be here at his side if it wasn't her? Because it couldn't be her.

His gaze found hers and he wiped his hands clean. "You're thinking hard."

She gave him a soft smile and withheld her thoughts. He was already hoping to change her mind into moving back home. As much as she was entertaining the idea, she just couldn't. *She couldn't.* Those reasons were there. Besides, this was her life she was flirting with changing on practically a whim. This wasn't like deciding whether or not to pick up bread from a gas station or take a trip to the grocery store so she could get toilet paper at the same time.

She pushed hair away from her face and glanced to him. "Just a long day."

He caught her by the wrist. She didn't resist as he tugged. As she landed on his lap, perhaps she should have. He'd wanted his recliner and a movie. Not a hard kitchen chair. Except there was kissing. A lot of kissing that was turning into grabbing and wanting and wrapping her arms around him.

Long kissing that took away the stress of her thoughts. If it was taking away her stress, no doubt it was easing his mind too. So for that, she should keep kissing, keep wrapping her arms around his neck as he stood and carried her out of the kitchen.

Finally, some good reason. Heart-pounding, skin-heating reasons that had her seeking out more and wanting to crawl under his shirt to be skin on skin. He pushed a door opened and stepped into his bedroom.

She vaguely took notice of the dark furniture, light spilling from a bathroom and the clothes on the bed that he brushed out of the way before laying her on it and coming down on top of her. He surrounded her senses, jumped her responses into overdrive. He grazed his fingers along her sides as her shirt came off and sent out trickling tingles to prick over her skin.

He moved his kiss from her lips to her chin, neck. She could barely catch her breath to keep up with him, but she made up time fast and had his shirt stripped off and landing somewhere across the room.

Hot skin touched hot skin. His heart against her breast pounded in time with hers. He feathered his lips over her neck. "If you don't want this, we can stop."

She squeezed her eyes shut and sent any sort of no-like response to the dark corner of her mind. Reasons to stop this from happening—reasons that she so far hadn't been able to define and were pointless to even attempt to figure out now. The touch of his lips against her neck, shoulder, back to her mouth, flicked chill bumps across her skin.

Life had always been about doing this or focusing on that. Coming here had changed everything. Being back in Turtle Pine for this simple job hadn't really made her think about the bigger picture for both her career and her life. Coming home had been all about finishing this one quick job and getting back to her life. It hadn't taken a whole lot of mental power.

At least until Cade. Because with him over her? Oh, yes, he was zapping all her attention and focusing it on nothing but him. She couldn't imagine being anywhere else in this moment. Even if presented with the chance to go to Texas right now, she wouldn't take that offer. Being here with Cade was the only place she wanted to be. Stopping wasn't an option. "I wouldn't be here if I didn't want this."

And that was the truth. The honest-to-goodness truth of this whole situation. She wanted this. Wanted this so damn bad. Going forward meant she was going to want him and this growing thing between them so damn much more. Even that wasn't enough to scare her into throwing on the brakes and getting out of here.

Instead, she had her hands on his pants and pushed them down. Going forward with this was going to make it so much harder to leave. As he got her pants off and was back over her in just his underwear, well, she was going to have to have someone tie her to the plane and let it drag her down the runway to get her to leave.

She couldn't imagine being done exploring him before it was time to pack up and leave. There were so many layers and interesting turns and sides of him. So much about him she wanted to explore and his body was just one of the many.

The way his shoulders flexed under her hands. The draw of his breath as he palmed her breast and tasted the other. Her toes curled as parts of her opened up for him, wanted more of him. What the hell, she wrapped around him and pulled him against her to get down and dirty faster. His length was firm at the parting of her thighs, rocking against her, taking her breath with every stroke coupled with his lips on her nipple.

His moans hummed against her chest, between her breasts as he turned and the scruff of his jaw grazed her skin. She wanted to touch him everywhere, at once. Have his mouth discover every last part of her. Learn the roughness of his chin against the inside of her thigh, his tongue against her body like he'd kissed her mouth.

All of it, now, in this one night. The tip of him on her lips, his shaft over her tongue.

This night was supposed to be for him, about him. A way to ease the long, rough day he'd had. The way she had it figured, they had three nights before she had to go. Tonight was for him. She planted her foot and pushed. He let her roll them and she was across his lap, straddling his hips. Her knees were in against his waist.

He lifted his brows as she got seated more comfortable, lowering more firmly over his length trapped between them. His hands went up her sides, caught her bare shoulders and pulled her over. Her mouth met his and the kiss returned. A heavy-breathing teeth-clashing devouring kiss. She sought his taste and kiss and wanted it imprinted in her memory as a souvenir of the night.

He gripped her hips and his tight hold put her right in a slow, achingly teasing rhythm she wanted. His fingers pinched into her sides as he shifted his legs, pulling away from her. She fought to keep him right where he was, with that steady rhythm. Taking it away would surely leave her dead.

"Annie," her name seemed to tear past his lips on a harsh whisper. "Nightstand."

She frowned and then realized…right, condoms. That was a temporary cold bucket of water to slow things down. With a long stretch, she got one between her fingertips from the drawer. There was no missing the tremble of his hands as he took the package from her. Yeah, okay. The night was still young with plenty of time for everything else she had in mind. Watching him fumble with the wrapper, she bit back a laugh and plucked it from him. "I think you're in need of some assistance."

"I've thought about this moment happening for a long time."

She ripped open the package. "Did it always include you turning into all thumbs?"

His laughter filled the room and warmed it. "Not even a little."

"Eh, things rarely turn out as we think. I think it makes it more fun."

The backs of his knuckles went down her sides. "You were always happy."

"You got that part right." She covered him and bent over for a kiss. If he was still nervous, she couldn't tell it in his kiss. His mouth commanded attention. His hands were in her hair and holding her to him. She slid off his lap. Holding tight to his shoulders, she pulled him with her.

His hips were between her thighs and his tip pressed to her opening. Slowly, his fullness stretched her. Her breath hitched and caught as he moved deeper. His eyes rolled back and his chest filled as he sank. She moved with him, getting used to his size. The gentle taking wouldn't last long. Not by the pounding of her pulse and the gripping need to move faster, harder, to pick up her pace and meet his demands. She gave over to the need—to what that they both wanted.

His grunts mixed with hers. A pulsing stream of tension filled her veins as he thrust over and over until she couldn't handle more. A grunt became a shout. All that tension flooded out and she stilled as he thrust. Then everything about everything she'd been stressing over didn't matter.

None of it mattered anymore. Where she lived, what this was about, what she'd spent years running from. There was only this that mattered. This moment between her and Cade that centered around everything she wanted, everything that could change on a dime as he wrapped his arms around her and held her tight. For a blissful, frozen moment in time, everything in the world was exactly as she could ever want it.

The feeling didn't last. All too quickly, reality came knocking. She curled her fingers in against his sides, snuggled in as close as possible and wanted to blink and magically find them somewhere else. A different time, a different place. Anywhere but here in Turtle Pine.

The moment of what exactly had just happened here—what she'd knowingly gone into with her eyes wide open—settled on her shoulders. What was worse was that she was tempted into wanting more. Way more than she had figured

Oh, geez.

Chapter Twelve

Cade parked among the full lot outside the bakery. Even his mom was here, which meant there would probably be two little kids running around. He pushed through the back door and found what looked like a town meeting surrounding the table.

Boxes were stacked in the center and Annie was right in the middle of it all. Their eyes met. Immediately, Annie's cheeks reddened. She looked back down as she worked. Not for long though, because she sent him a look through her lashes, then she was head back down, spinning more frosting over the lined-out cupcakes.

The glance should have been an innocent look, but it landed on him and sent his mind right to this morning. Water had been pouring over him when she'd closed her hot mouth around him. He'd managed not to fall in the shower as she'd turned his world upside down. Once the water cleared from his eyes, he saw her on her knees before him, his length in her mouth and her gaze on him. That had been the end of him.

Annie-Lyn had given him head. It was a wonder he hadn't passed out. From the moment he'd gotten her text yesterday, it'd been one continual dream come true after another. He'd been afraid to fall asleep last night in fear he'd wake up and find it all had been another dream. Instead, the morning dregs in his eyes had cleared away to the feel of her wrapped in his arms and moaning at the alarm clock.

The plan had been to drop her off at her grandparents' early, but by the time he'd stumbled out the shower and bent her over the bathroom sink, there hadn't been time for all that. She'd put on her shorts from yesterday and slipped on one of his old high school shirts that hung off her in all the best possible ways.

Now to figure out how to get her back for the night again, then the next night and the one after that, until *the next* became forever. How could something that felt so right not happen? He had to find a way to make her stay and was running short on time to get that done.

A white bag was in her hands and she hovered over a row of cupcakes. He watched, realizing they were working an assembly line. His mom was lining out cupcakes, Annie was frosting them, a couple guys from the mechanic shop were folding up boxes and her grandpa was coming up last, boxing the cupcakes while another guy from the mechanic shop was stacking.

He had no idea where the kids were. He couldn't help but chuckle and knew for sure that Annie was the source the efficiency. "Need another set of hands?"

All four guys who worked at the mechanic shop had an arm up in an instant. Annie laughed. "Nobody's going anywhere. Wash up and help Grandpa. We don't have but a couple hundred left."

Cade washed up and got in place. The efficiency line kicked in a little faster. "Where are the kids?"

"TV room," his mom answered.

Annie's grandpa looked extra proud. "I've done this a time or two with a kid underfoot."

After fifty or so cupcakes moved past him, Cade was feeling like he'd done this a time or two also. As much as his back was starting to ache and everyone—except Annie—took a break, Cade stuck it out. He wanted to be in there with her and hopefully his help would get them done faster and he'd manage a little bit of extra time with her.

His mom lined out a tray and announced it was the last one. The feeling in the room lifted with a chorus of everything from, "Thank God," to heavy releases of breaths. Cade closed the last box, put it with the stack and everyone stood around, eyes on Annie. She searched them all and the biggest, most satisfied grin spread out on her face. "Let's load up. Careful not to tip the boxes."

Eventually, every last inch of floorboard space, trunk and laps of passengers were full. Even still, there were stacks left inside waiting to be loaded.

She rubbed the back of her neck. "Let's get over to the school and as a car gets unloaded, we'll head back and refill."

"Sounds like a plan." Having her ride shotgun with him would be a plan too, but she had her grandpa's car loaded and was driving that one. He wasn't sure how many trips went back and forth between the bakery and the school.

Annie, his mom, the kids and he stayed at the school so they could make the longer walk from the parking lot to the office while her grandpa and his friends did most of the driving. He walked in behind Annie, placing another box in the long hall while the kids were all in class.

The principal looked at the stacks and stacks lining the hall and chuckled. "Goodness. I can't thank you enough."

Annie lifted her shoulders and then rubbed her hands off on her pants. "Happy to help."

Cade rocked on his heels. "Isn't there a pep rally today?" At the principal's nod, he went on. "Maybe point her out to the kids as the one who made the cupcakes?" A gym full of kids cheering her was surely a great way to show that living here would be different than before.

"No, that's not—" Annie tried getting out of it, but she wasn't fast enough. Her eyes were wide with looked like terror and oh, shit. Cade had a feeling he'd be paying for this idea later.

The principal was grinning ear to ear. "I love that." She stopped and clasped her hands together. "Or, better yet, since this was about the football field, let's do it there instead. Can you come tonight?"

Annie's eyes were the size of bowling balls now. Well, he wanted more time with her. Having her for a date at the football game fell right in line with more things he wanted. These dreams he had of them included stuff like Friday night football games. He never imagined Annie looking terrified about it though. The principal stared at her, awaiting a response. He bumped Annie with his elbow. "Sounds like fun. I'd love to have a date tonight."

Annie's gaze moved to him and she shrugged. "All right."

"Wonderful." The principal pulled up her sleeves. "Now to get these delivered. If y'all don't have anything to do, you're welcome to stick around and help."

They both got busy again, grabbing a stack of boxes and taking them to the kindergarteners. Their classrooms were down the long, quiet hallway. It left Cade all alone with Annie for a few moments.

She gave him a quick side-eye, but there was still a little smile with it. "Suggesting the principal to point me out at the pep rally? And now the football game? I was starting to fall for you, Cade Revlin, but not so much anymore."

"Ouch. You're breaking my heart here." He chuckled. "I guess you'll have to stay with me tonight so I can spend the evening making it up to you."

By the color that went across her cheeks, he was pretty confident he'd nailed that. She cleared her throat but they reached their classroom before she could answer him. Back and forth they went for an hour delivering cupcakes to classrooms, listening to cheers and watching dancing kids. Big grins with frosting-covered mouths shouting thank yous to high schoolers slamming their books closed with a yelled *yes*.

Annie didn't stop beaming through any of it. All he wanted to do was spin her behind a brick column or maybe drag her out to the sparse standing of trees where the high school kids took break and kiss her senseless. Anywhere to get her alone and back to as close as they'd been last night.

They walked side by side out the front of the school. Her hand swung next to his and he couldn't help himself. He grabbed hers and interlocked their fingers. For his efforts, she gave him a raised brow.

But she didn't pull away. Instead, she chuckled. "This doesn't make up for what you've roped me into tonight."

"On the upside, now I don't have to try and talk you into going to the game later." He guessed that she would have preferred to avoid going where he knew good and well her sisters, along with everyone else in Turtle Pine, would be tonight.

She nodded. "Right. You'll be there working?"

"Not officially, but it's expected. I'll be off, but I'll be parked there with my car and be in uniform to make sure there's no trouble."

He walked her the last few feet to the parking lot and pulled open her car door. Dang it, why hadn't he caught her grandpa and asked the man to drive the car out of here? Then Cade could have had Annie with him. His time was running out.

She stood in the doorway with one foot in the car and her arms resting casually over the top of the open door. "Can you pick me up or do I need to meet you there?"

"I'll pick you up." Would actually love to do that.

"I didn't know if it was okay to ride in the cop car."

He rested his hands on the door on either side of her. "Be no trouble at all."

Afraid to put too much thought into it, he leaned over and left a fast kiss on her cheek, like it was casual and normal and that it happened all the time. That's exactly what the kiss felt like as he pulled back from her pinked cheeks. It was an easy, uncomplicated kiss. Something that felt so natural and right, like it happened all the time and more would come later. "See you around six."

She blinked and managed a nod as she slipped in her car. He pushed the door closed. Instead of driving off to do nothing, he moved his car to a more displayed spot in front of the school and headed back in as students filled the gym for the pep rally. After thunderous stomping and cheers and introductions in a hot gym that set his head spinning, it finally let out.

He took position by the side of the road and clicked his lights on to encourage the traffic to slow it down. The time couldn't possibly drag by any slower. He knew the opposite was going to happen when he saw Annie again, that the time would somehow jump into overdrive. Before he knew it, it was going to be morning again and he'd have to start letting her go.

Then he'd somehow face the fact that he was going to have to say goodbye. Not just for a few hours like this morning. But as far as he knew, for forever. Maybe he'd see her every couple years. Maybe. Still felt like forever.

He dropped paperwork by the office and thankfully, by the time he got back to town it was close enough for him to pick her up. Five-fifteen was close enough, right? He sure as hell hoped so as he pulled in the driveway at her grandparents'. The car she'd been driving was home, so at least he hadn't beaten her back here.

He made it halfway up the porch steps when the front door opened. Her grandma was there, beaming at him. "Cade!" Her arms went up in the air. "Cade Revlin!"

She announced it so loud and determined. He nearly thought he was in trouble for something, except her grin was a mile wide. She brought him in for a hug and patted his back. "How have you been?"

"Ah, pretty good, ma'am." And worried. Very worried about his near future.

She didn't get her hands off him. Instead, she caught him by the arm so he could escort her inside. Except she all but tugged him through the door to the kitchen table where she pointed at a chair. "Have a seat. Do you want a snack?"

Mr. Cookie looked over the paper. He lifted a bushy, gray and brown brow and searched the room before he snapped the paper shut. "What are you doing?"

She spun around and placed cookies down in the middle of the table. A glass of milk was quick to appear next. "I'm making Cade feel at home." She gave him another grin and touched his wrist. "Do you need anything else?"

Possibly a trip to reality somewhere. "I think you've got me more than taken care of here."

With a flourish and flick of her wrist, she sat at the table. "Annie got in the shower a minute or so ago." Her grandma didn't seem to be talking to her husband further and she plucked a cookie up and looked at it as she kept going. "I told her an hour ago to be getting cleaned up, that it wouldn't do to keep you waiting."

Cade cleared his throat, still trying to catch up from the moment she'd swept him in the door. "That's all right. I'm early."

"That's good." She kept grinning and added a glance his way. "I heard you helped at the school with the cupcakes."

He nodded. "Yes, ma'am. Happy to lend a hand."

"Good. I love that you're getting to spend some time with Annie."

Red alert. Was he about to get slit open for taking Annie away from spending time with her grandparents? He hadn't even considered he was monopolizing all her time. He cleared his throat. "I'm enjoying it too. I hope you didn't have plans that I've interfered with."

"Oh, of course not. Spend some more time together."

Mr. Cookie's eyes appeared over the newspaper again and narrowed in on his wife. "What are you going on about?"

"Nothing," she said none too innocently. "Just having a nice chat is all. Put that paper down and join us."

He muttered something. Cade didn't catch it, but by the quick side-eye she gave the older man, Cade was glad he didn't. Then she was back to being perky again. "So what are you and Annie doing this evening? Aside from the game."

"I'm not sure." He cleared his throat again. This milk needed to be traded in for something a lot stouter. It'd been a while since he'd been in a hot seat. "I'll try not to have her out late again."

"Oh, don't worry about that. Keep her out as late as you want. Keep her all night again if you want."

"Ruth." Her husband shot her a look.

She only glared back. "Well, what do you want me to do?"

"Stay out of it, that's what."

She made a spitting-like noise at him. It was something Cade had never in his life seen a woman of her age do before. He nearly lost it to a fit of laughter that would no doubt have him rolling on the floor if he gave in. She turned back to Cade. "You're both adults. It's not like I'm going to police her comings and goings. She's responsible. If she wants to sleep over with you again, that would be great."

His parents had never covered etiquette like this before. Be respectful. Use your manners. Smile. All those? Yep, his dad had made sure Cade had those down. Proper response to your date's grandparents pleading you to take their granddaughter home for the night? Nope, never covered that one.

Her grandpa leaned on the table. "I'm starting to worry about what *your* plans are tonight since you're trying to get rid of her."

"Get rid of her?" she all but shrieked. "I'm trying to keep her here. At home, where she belongs."

The older man still looked confused and muttered something else.

She grunted for a response. "She's obviously not going to move back home for us or she would have been back already. But if she falls in love, then she'll come back." Her gaze was back to Cade now. "I ran into your momma at Jasper's and we had a wonderful chat." She patted his hand. "I always thought you were a good boy."

How he would thank his mom for this later. Her grandpa was still confused, but Cade was catching on. "Don't sell yourself short. She mentioned that she would like to be here to take care of you two and be here as you need her."

"It's not enough. She would be back if that's what she wanted. When she left, I never dreamed she would be gone this long."

"It's complicated," Cade gave for an excuse.

"Something with her and Jane." She sighed. "I know. That's why I hoped she'd do Jane's cake. Bygones would be bygones."

He was starting to see a bigger picture now. One that didn't have a nagging grandma just trying to guilt trip Annie, but a loving grandma who was grasping at straws. If his heart wasn't already hurting enough at the thought of Annie leaving, it just kinked into painful throbs. The way Mrs. Cookie was staring at him, it looked like she was placing all her hope on his head.

That wasn't a good idea. "Don't get your hopes up on me."

"You're my best shot."

"I can't make her stay."

"I know." Her gaze trailed off. "But you have more of a shot of changing her mind than anyone."

No, he would wager Jane would have a better shot. Cade didn't care what it took, tonight he was going to have to corner Jane somehow when Annie wasn't looking and get her to talk to her sister. With the principal planning to recognize her at the game, Cade was just going to have to make sure she was *recognized* well and good. Like at halftime on the fifty-yard line so he'd have plenty of time to pull Jane off to the side and beg the girl to make amends with Annie. There's no way he could convince Jane over the phone, and he certainly couldn't leave Annie right now to go find her. Halftime was his best option.

Chapter Thirteen

Annie rested against the front of Cade's cop car next to him, feeling for all the world like she belonged there. The last time she'd been on this field, it had been to walk across the grass and get her diploma. She'd been out there and off as fast as she could to get it over with. In about ten or so minutes, she'd get to walk across that grass again.

And give a speech. Because she'd made some cupcakes. If someone had to go out there, it should be her grandpa, since it had been his idea. Or maybe Cade, since he'd gotten her into this mess. Her throat tightened. It wasn't that she was shy. College graduation had been massive, and she would have danced across the stage there if they'd let her.

This was Turtle Pine. She was about to be center field in the town she'd spent years hiding and running from. All because of Cade.

He readjusted his stance. "I see you looking at me like that."

"You ought to. I'm not hiding my feelings."

He chuckled, and even considering the situation, she couldn't help but fall for the sound a little. "You'll be great. It'll be fun and over before you know it."

She crossed her arms over her chest. "I expect you to remember this later tonight. You have a lot of making up to do."

That caught his attention. "You'll come home with me tonight?"

She looked up in thought. "I'm thinking for a back massage,

breakfast in bed and whatever else I can think up between now and then. Yeah, I'll be there."

As if there was ever any question that she wasn't going home with him. All she had left was tonight and tomorrow night. That was it. Her plane even left Sunday morning, so Sunday didn't even count as a day. She was supposed to somehow get her fill of everything she wanted over what, the next thirty-six hours?

She'd all but chewed her lip off trying to figure out how that was going to work. The whistle blew and it was showtime. Cade kissed her on the cheek. Smooth and easy and it just felt like it belonged. "Kill 'em, honey."

She hunted down the principal on the sidelines. That's where they were supposed to meet and thankfully walk out together so she wouldn't have to do this by herself. Seeing as she'd spent all her high school years trying to avoid any sort of spotlight at this school, she didn't want to think about having to face these people on her own.

She wasn't that same girl. She was independent with a successful life that she was darn proud of. Annie couldn't help but scope for a fast way out as the last of the football players walked by her. As soon as the last athlete had disappeared under the stands for the path to the locker room, she spotted the principal.

The woman rubbed her hands as they got close. "Are you ready?"

If ready meant she was about to pee her pants, then sure, Annie was totally ready. "As ready as I'm going to be."

The woman laughed. "It'll be fun."

Oh, how many different definitions the word fun must have. Not that Annie could change how any of this was going down. They marched out on the field as the bands gathered on the sidelines, waiting on them to get out of the way.

They walked all the way out to the very center of the field. Not just partway where they would have been seen fine, but *all* the way to the middle. Annie's throat was tighter than a springform pan snapped into place as the principal introduced her to the crowd and pointed out their spiffed-up field.

Cheers rang out. Towels or flags—they were too far away for Annie to tell—waved from the stands and the microphone was shoved at her. She managed a swallow as the crowd quieted and everyone stared.

Somebody somewhere coughed, and it was time to do this. "I'm delighted to be back home for the first game of the season this year. You guys did a great job cleaning up the field. I heard kindergarteners to seniors all took part in some way. I don't think it looked this good when I went to school here."

Cheers erupted again, so clearly she was on the right path with this thing. "While I may have baked the reward for all the students this week, the real credit should go to my grandpa for coming up with the idea and to everyone who took part in getting our field ready. Y'all had the hard work and all of you did a wonderful job. Now let's beat those Bobcats!"

There were more cheers, the microphone was out of her hands and she was running as the principal led her off the field. She got to the sidelines and the principal caught her by her elbow. "You might want to wait here."

Annie looked up and found the band right in her path.

"Trust me, you do not want to run between the drum major and the band. I did that once. Never again."

Annie laughed and stepped back, sitting on the bench the players had vacated. A huge weight lifted off her shoulders. She'd survived and could high-five every one of the band members marching by. "I guess I get a front-row seat for the program then?"

She nodded. "I think it's better from the stands because you can see down, but there's nobody here who might spill popcorn or soda all over you."

Now that she'd gotten her speech out of the way, some of that salty popcorn sounded like a plan. Come on, third quarter. Her stomach let out a rumble, agreeing with that exact thought.

The visiting band performed their number. Flashing colors of red and gold and big plumes danced off their hats until they marched in smart, straight lines off the field so the home team could come on and do their number. She glanced down the field, trying to spy Cade, but he wasn't in front of his car parked behind the goal post.

Hopefully, he was getting her some of that popcorn he'd offered her in the first half. The band played for several minutes. The majorettes danced in front of them and each time their batons went up in the air, Annie's breathing stopped and didn't start back up until the wands were safely caught.

A loud, attention-demanding rhythm hit the drums and the crowd yelled once again as they finished. The band marched off the field, blocking her. She fell in step behind, caught up in their uniform marching and somewhat slow pace until they finally reached the edge of the stands and her path was clear. People swirled around each other. Kids ran everywhere and a teenage girl's annoying laugh sounded out. Through all that, Annie found somewhat of a smile.

As the football players made their way back onto the field, the line at the concession stand that was six deep turned and watched them. Familiar faces were everywhere, but Annie had been such a loner. She settled in against the front of Cade's car and returned small waves and smiles and slight nods at people she could faintly put names to.

People who had kids running around next to them. Others with babies. A lot of them looked like they'd never left, never missed a game at this field—only gotten a little older. Maybe they had never left.

The whistle blew, the clock started and within seconds, the ball was snapped before a crowd with hopeful, held breaths.

A flag was thrown out and Cade was back at her side, handing over a bag of popcorn. He smiled her way, but it looked tight. "Thought you might be ready for this now."

She took the bag, but didn't eat any yet. "Is everything okay? You look mad about something. Or frustrated."

He blinked and all traces of the strain disappeared. "Just, um, there were some kids causing trouble in line."

"Thanks for dealing with the teens and getting the popcorn. Now that halftime is over, I'm getting hungry." She rubbed his arm and he relaxed further next to her, resting back on the hood of the car.

"Give it about five minutes and the concession will clear out and we can grab hot dogs."

"Hot dogs and popcorn." She found herself ridiculously smiling.

"Is something wrong? If you want to wait, we can grab something after the game. I need to stick around though until after most everyone is gone."

She stared into her paper bag of over-salted cold popcorn. "No, it's great actually. Everything is really great." She looked up to him and lifted a shoulder. "I never did this before."

"That's what happens when you spend all your time trying to avoid people."

"I know." She rested her head on his shoulder in the middle of all these people and felt totally comfortable about doing it. "But I didn't know what I was missing. I knew what I thought I was missing, but listening to the crowd yell and smelling the popcorn, it's more than I expected."

He wrapped his arm around her shoulders and gave her warm hug. "Just think, basketball starts in a few months, and you didn't really get to do that either, did you?"

She shook her. "Nope."

He tipped his head to the side. "Then baseball later on."

She chuckled. "Nope there too."

"With those things coming up to experience, I don't see how you can leave."

"I don't know how I can either." And not because of the ball games. How was she supposed to leave everything? How much longer could she keep saying that her job and her life was perfect and exactly how she wanted it? The lines of perfect she'd always drawn in the sand were getting more than a little blurry.

"Annie!"

Before she could even spin around, a little girl was attached to her leg. She flicked hair out of Katie's eyes. "What are you doing here?"

"Nana's getting me some candy."

Cade's mom appeared. "Just what she needs too."

"I'm sure it is."

Penny pointed at Katie. "She saw you over here and had to come see you."

Annie reached down and gave the girl a tight hug. "I sure am glad you did."

Cupcakes and Crushes

The little girl looked up, wide grin on her face. "Are you coming to lunch tomorrow?"

She hummed, trying to figure out a suitable answer. "I'm not sure."

Her eyes got bigger and she whipped her head around as she spoke, "But you *have* to. So we can play again."

"We'll see."

"And Nana's cooking—" the little girl squinted and looked to the woman in question, "—what did you say?"

"Pork chops."

"Pork chops," Katie repeated. "Nana's are the best. And then we can play."

Annie wasn't in the habit of accepting an invitation given by a four-year-old. "We'll see."

Cade bumped her with his arm. "I forgot to mention that Mom asked if you wanted to come for lunch tomorrow."

She sent him a glance. "Thanks for that."

"My pleasure. I don't think you'll be able to refuse that face."

She looked down and laughed as pleading eyes stared up at her. "I don't think I can refuse. I guess I will see you tomorrow."

"Yay!" Katie released the life-or-death grip on her thighs. "Uncle Peter said he was bringing cans, Uncle Cade."

His hands went up. "I'll get the Cricket and we'll go hunting. I promise."

And with that, Katie and Penny were off, taking Annie's breath with them. Peter? "Peter?"

He rubbed the back of his neck. "You know before how I mentioned that Mom likes to cook Sunday lunch?"

"Yeah."

"Since the wedding is Sunday, Mom is doing lunch on Saturday instead. A kind of good meal before the rehearsal tomorrow night."

Thoughts were supposed to be coming out of her opening and closing mouth. "You let Katie ask me. You didn't tell me Peter and Jane were going to be there before so I could come up with a reason why I couldn't be there."

He searched her face and then his brows softened. "No, honey." He rubbed her lower back. "I swear I forgot. You know I wouldn't corner you like that on purpose."

"I don't know. I hate to back out after I've told Katie yes."

"Peter will be there, but Jane isn't supposed to be. She's working at the church all day. And Peter isn't going to bother you, I promise. I'll be with you the whole time. If I'm not, then I know Katie will be keeping you entertained. Or Kent. Or Mom. I'll make sure Peter doesn't get you cornered. I don't think he would anyway. If it'll make you feel better, I can talk to him ahead of time."

She didn't want Cade going around making people play nice with her. She could be a big girl when she had to be and she could survive a Saturday lunch. Surviving it seemed a far better option over missing it.

He rubbed her arms. "I wouldn't throw you to the wolves. Ever."

She bit her lip and sighed. "I'm sorry."

"Give me some credit, okay?"

She nodded. "I know. I'm sorry." She looked up. "Forgive me?"

"I guess."

"I suppose we're even now."

"I don't mind giving the back massage still."

She bit at her lip for different reasons. "I like the sound of that."

"I like the idea of you volunteering to do breakfast in bed in the morning."

She was laughing again as they turned and faced the game. "I suppose I can manage that."

"Nothing heavy though. You heard Katie. Mom is making pork chops, and I don't want to be too full for that."

Chapter Fourteen

Cade walked with his arm over Annie's shoulders as the last few talkers were hopefully wrapping up. If it had been anyone else besides the parents of the starting quarterback, tight end and defensive end of the JV squad, Cade would have been fine leaving them. But Cade knew full well how the three sets of parents—who were close friends—could get sidetracked talking and not pay attention to their often into-everything kids. He'd been setting those three boys straight on what was okay to touch and what wasn't since they were in kindergarten and he'd first gotten this job. They were at the age where their curiosity was starting to be called vandalism. Man, next year they'd be in high school. He was getting old.

Not just old, but old with not a lot to show for it other than his career. Annie could change all that. Take his single life and turn it into so much more. A wife, kids. He found his gaze straying across the playground to the set of parents talking about whatever. That could be him and Annie one day. He found his gaze straying elsewhere to the three boys sitting on a bench. One of those kids could be theirs.

It wasn't going to happen though. He'd spent the whole halftime pleading with Jane to talk to Annie. He'd kept pleading even as the band had left the field and he'd caught sight of Annie heading back to where they'd been standing. Jane hadn't budged though. She'd said she wished she could talk to Annie, but they had some sort of silent truce that she wasn't breaking. That was why Jane was skipping Saturday lunch. Not because of some wedding details. Jane was way too organized to wait to the last minute for anything. She was skipping Saturday lunch to avoid Annie. She was afraid if she showed up Annie would leave, and she didn't want to be the cause of Annie running anymore.

Even though Cade had told Jane if they would talk, it could be enough to get Annie to stay, she hadn't believed him. So as the parents talked, he sat on the swing next to Annie at the playground and tried really hard not to count the hours down until it was time to say goodbye.

She pushed off the ground, swinging herself a little and stealing glances back and forth. Her swing slowed and she twisted in a circle, twining the chains all the way to her lap.

She leaned against the tangled chains holding her seat. "So this is a typical Friday night for you?"

His heart was heavy, but he put effort into not showing it. He didn't want to remember being in a sour mood and wasting what time was left. "It is during football season. For home games only. It depends on where the away game is and if I'm working that Friday if I can be there. Pretty simple, huh?"

"That's the part I like about it."

"All this could be yours."

She was quiet and he was almost sorry for letting that slight bitterness slip out, but a long breath eased out of her. "I didn't think it was possible, but you are making a tempting, tempting offer."

"All the cold, salty popcorn you could ever want, right here at your fingertips."

"Sweet talker." There was a flash of a grin and she lifted her feet and the chains un-spiraled from the tight wrap she'd made.

The twisting slowed and he caught her by the knees and faced her to him. If they had a little more privacy, he'd kiss her. But he was pretty sure he'd gotten onto all the three of the boys for doing that sort of thing. Instead, he settled for rubbing his thumbs along her the insides of her knees. "Can I at least talk you into coming back and visiting?"

"Possibly." She sighed and her eyes dropped closed. "I wish I lived closer," she whispered.

"So do I."

"To get here in a decent amount of time, it's a plane ride. Not even a quick one. No direct flights to Houston. I have to drive to Dallas. It makes it harder to visit. Or for you to visit me."

"You name the day and I'll do my best to be knocking on your door."

"Every day."

Damn it, this sucked so much. "Don't be surprised if you catch me surfing the Internet later to see what jobs there are in your area."

"You can't leave here."

"I think I could." He would miss it. He'd never wanted to leave home, but in time, maybe the missing would dull. After all, he would have her.

"What about your mom?" she asked.

"She would want me happy."

"Your brother? Your sister? Katie?"

Katie. She would be the hard one to leave. He didn't know what having kids was like. He'd heard Beth say it was a love that couldn't be explained, only experienced. He'd like to think he was as close to Katie as a person could be. He loved that little girl. Yeah, Annie was right. Extra weight piled on his breaking heart. "I can't leave."

She rested her elbows on her thighs and rubbed his arms. "I know. I would never ask you to, and deep inside, you really don't want to."

"Is that how you feel about moving back here?" He pushed a hand over the top of his head. He'd known she hadn't wanted to move here, but he'd never considered her moving home was equal to the level of dislike he had for leaving.

She gave his question thought as she studied him. "It was when I got here. If not worse."

"And now?"

She pushed her swing back into motion. "And now, I don't know. I'm confused."

"Allow me to unconfuse you."

She laughed. "You're the reason I'm confused to begin with." She lifted a shoulder. "If not for you, I would have slipped into town, done my work and left."

"It feels like I should apologize for some reason, but I'm not going to."

He got a smile out of her for that. "I don't want you to either. I'm just a little torn on what I want."

"I know exactly what I want." He tipped his head toward the people still talking. "For them to leave so I can get you home again."

She smiled. "I'm not confused on that, because it sounds great."

"And you promised me breakfast in bed. I don't want to miss that."

"Don't forget my back massage." She shot back.

"I wouldn't dare." He traced the turn of her arm down to her waist. "I'm thinking of getting you naked so there won't be any clothes in my way."

She cleared her throat. "You make a good point."

"Get you sprawled and comfortable across my bed."

"Definitely," she was down to a whisper.

With a heavy sigh, he looked at the parents still clustered together. "Maybe if we walk to my car, it'll stir them into getting out of here."

"I like that plan. Too bad about all that equipment and stuff between the front seats of the car."

He groaned and stood. Too bad about all that stuff indeed. He caught her hand in his and they walked across the narrow sidewalk to where his car was still parked behind a goal post. As he opened the passenger door for her, he was relieved to see the set of parents breaking apart and heading for their cars.

He settled in behind the wheel as the cars finally started up and pulled out of the lot in a line. He got in behind them and turned for home. Again he was struck with how much he liked the feel of this. With her in the car beside him, them going home together. It wasn't her home, but it could be. Maybe not the house he currently lived in. It was starting to feel a little cursed with Tina next door.

Besides, his house wasn't built for a family. It was a two-bedroom place. Not near enough room for two kids. Or maybe three. And where was the dog supposed to go? No yard at all. There had to be a yard. Not just for the dog, but he needed somewhere to play catch with his kids.

He found himself turning left at the stop sign.

She glanced his way. "Have something you need to check on?"

"Just a quick drive through before going home." And that's what it was. But not for any purpose or reason she might be thinking. Maple Street was as quiet as he'd expected, even still, as he reached the center of the strip, he slowed at the brick house that still had the for-sale sign in the front. Slowed…and then stopped.

"Do you see something?"

Just a house that was perfect. There was even a tree house in the backyard. "I wanted to check this house." He cleared his throat. "Kids can be rowdy Friday night after the first game. Want to make sure no one is making use of this empty house for any sort of gathering."

"Ah." She settled in her seat, but a quick glance over told him that she was still studying the house. "That's, ah, ah." She snapped her fingers. "The…Normans used to live there?"

"The Butlers."

She chuckled. "So wasn't even close. When did they move?"

"Over the summer. Their oldest graduated and they headed north to retire."

She settled in against her seat. "Always thought it was a pretty house."

"Me too." He let his foot off the brake and this time headed for home. His home that would be empty in a matter of days. Heck, at this point, he could say hours. This was nothing more than torture.

He needed to get his head wrapped around saying goodbye instead of dreaming up ideas that weren't going to happen. He wasn't changing her mind. Really, it was ridiculous to think it was even possible.

Tina's house was lit up next door but he was confident now that she wasn't going to come out after him. He supposed, if anything, at least maybe this week he'd had with Annie had gotten Tina off his back. He'd take Tina on every day if it meant keeping Annie though.

Annie rubbed his arm. "You okay? You've gotten really quiet since we got in the car."

No, he wasn't okay. He didn't want to say that and drag this night down. He tried his best to give a reassuring smile, but he doubted he'd succeeded. He patted her hands instead. "Glad to be home, I guess."

By the way she studied him, her eyes narrowing at the corners and gaze sweeping him down and back up, he didn't figure she bought it. She kept up the charade of things being okay and reached for the door handle. "Come on. Maybe I should give you the back massage."

He breathed and followed her inside. There was that to look forward to tonight. He barely got in the doorway and her arms were around his neck. He dropped his keys to the floor and kicked the door closed. The only reason she wasn't up in his arms yet was because he turned back to flip the locks.

After that she was all his. He took her to his room to get the most out of this night that he possibly could. He had two nights left to squeeze a lifetime into and he aimed to see that done.

Hot kisses led to stripped clothes. Naked skin against naked skin as they rolled over his sheets from one place to another until they were combined. It was only the beginning on this epic long night.

If there weren't bags under his eyes come morning, he'd done something wrong. Her soft moans mingled with his harder grunts as though they'd been made for the purpose of doing this together. Thrust after thrust, her nails scraping his back, he kept it going until he couldn't hold back anymore.

Breathless, he came down on top of her and rested on his elbows. Hot pants of air fanned over his cheeks and then a short laugh came out with it. She pushed hair back from her face that was beginning to get sweaty. "Oh my goodness."

He dropped a kiss between her brows. "Give me a second to get cleaned up and I'll start on that back rub."

Her hands went over his shoulder. A smooth rub of hot palms on him sent his nerves to lick all the way to his toes. Her nails caught the short hairs of his neck. "I thought we'd changed it so that I was giving you the massage?"

"We can do that later."

A brow went up. "Does that mean we're both cooking breakfast come morning?"

Now that was a picture he liked. Her in his shirt. Maybe in panties, maybe not, as she flipped a pancake and he stood next to her turning bacon. He pressed another kiss on her. "I think it does."

Chapter Fifteen

During Annie's senior year of college, she started working full-time at the bakery while carrying her full class load to graduate on time. She'd lived off coffee and been fine. She had a feeling she could drink the world's largest pot today and still feel dragged down.

Cade parked to the side at his mom's house and she tested a hand through her hair to find it was mostly dry. They'd fallen asleep around four this morning and slept until eleven. He'd forgone a shower to give her time to take one and thrown on a ball cap to hide the hair she'd spent half the night getting her hands in. She'd borrowed a shirt to wear over her jeans so she wouldn't walk in wearing the same thing as yesterday and had dried her hair in the wind on the drive over.

After the rush of running to make it in time for lunch, she hadn't considered the fact that she would be seeing Peter until now. Until now that his red Jeep was parked next to Cade's. The one she'd lost her virginity in and had thought she'd found herself pregnant in. Oh boy.

"Hey." Cade rubbed her leg. "It's going to be fine."

She breathed in. Yep, still felt more sick than reassured. "Logically, I know that."

"In a minute, your heart will catch up to what your head already knows."

At that point, the front door opened and Katie came running out to them. Seeing the little girl had the churn slowing down in her belly. She could do this. She had the complete attention of a four-year-old to keep her busy.

"Annie!"

She pushed out the car door and met the girl who stopped suddenly and frowned at her with a cock of her head. "How come you're wearing Uncle Cade's shirt?"

Cade chuckled as he rounded the front fender. He covered his mouth and didn't look like he planned to rescue her anytime soon. Annie cleared her throat and had the girl up on her hip. "Well, mine was dirty. Thankfully, Cade said I could borrow this one."

Katie looked serious. "Be careful in it. That's his *favorite* shirt."

Annie took a second glance at the old shirt advertising a marathon. He'd tossed it to her and she'd figured it was what he'd grabbed first. But on a second look, she could see that the colors were well faded. The cotton on her shoulders was soft with wear. "Well then, I'll be extra careful."

She stepped in the house and it took about two seconds before she was faced with Peter. He wasn't as tall as she remembered. Or maybe she was taller now. His hair was darker but he still had that dimple to the left of his smile and dark, dark eyes.

He gave her a little smile and pushed his hands in his pocket. "Hi, Annie."

"Hi," she managed. Everything was starting to get bunchy in her stomach, but then Katie wrapped her arms around Annie's neck and laid her head on her shoulder, and just like that, Annie felt better. She could so do this. It was one lunch.

Katie gave her a squeeze. "Can I sit by you at lunch?"

Annie patted the girl's bottom. "You sure can."

With that, she wiggled down and left Annie high and dry, but as Cade had promised, he was there, arm over her shoulder. Her throat was thick as she stared at Peter for a few seconds longer. Long enough that it started getting a little awkward. What exactly were you supposed to say to someone you'd spent years avoiding? "Congratulations."

He lifted his brow. "Thanks. Tomorrow is the big day. You coming?"

"Y'all didn't invite me."

He winced and rubbed the back of his neck. "Sorry. I didn't do the invitations."

And with that, she found herself laughing. "No, I'm sorry. Jane's perfected the art of letting me be. I'm not bitter that I wasn't invited."

He winced again "She wanted me to tell you hi if I saw you. She's busy getting ready for tonight."

Annie nodded. "Pass on my congratulations."

Cade rubbed her arm. "I think Mom was going to make a cake. If it goes in the oven, she tends to forget about it."

And there was her exit. Thank goodness. "I'm on it."

As she walked away, this weight that had been there before was gone. That actually hadn't been so bad at all. Peter had looked more terrified than she'd felt. Annie passed through the doorway to the kitchen.

Why had she always imagined Jane and Peter looking superior and on top of the world? She'd always felt so small and like she was being laughed at. That wasn't the way it'd gone at all. Penny was in full swing with last details in the kitchen and Annie jumped in with her.

Annie turned with a bowl for salad and a tall woman who looked at a lot like a younger version of Penny walked in. She could only be one person. Annie grinned her way. "Beth?"

Beth's gaze found hers and she came across the kitchen. "Annie! Oh my goodness, you're all grown up."

Annie set the bowl down just in time as Beth gave her a hug. "I can't believe how you've changed."

Annie laughed. "I was probably fifteen last you saw me."

Beth nodded. "I guess so. Thanks for letting the kids in the bakery. Katie has talked about you nonstop. I think I've even heard Kent trying to say your name."

Oh, now that smacked her right in the center of her chest. "They're sweet kids."

After a whirlwind of dishes and laughter, Annie was around the table. Food that had been arranged with care and placed on the table was gone. Bellies were patted and the last of the sweet tea was finished. Katie pushed her empty plate away and told her about a cartoon with dogs and cats on TV. Annie had never seen the show, but Katie had clearly seen it at least five times a day.

Cade pushed away from the table. "All right, squirt. Are we going hunting or not?"

That was it for the movie talk. Katie was out of her chair in a flash and the boys were out the back door and setting up for their practice.

Beth sat back in her chair. "I think she would go with you anywhere. How long are you in town for? Maybe I can sucker you—I mean, talk you into babysitting."

Annie laughed. "I'm leaving tomorrow."

Beth frowned. "So soon?"

"Afraid so." Seriously afraid so. Getting more scared by the moment. She found her gaze straying to the back door where Cade had disappeared through. She was terrified of what she was leaving behind.

The door opened and they all waited to see who'd come back in for what, but it wasn't one of the boys who walked in. It was Jane.

And Annie was paralyzed. Actually, the whole room seemed to be.

Penny recovered the fastest. "Jane!" Penny stood. "Peter said not to expect you. Let me make you a space to sit."

Jane waved her off with a quick flick of her wrist to stop her. "Thank you, but I'm not hungry." Her blue eyes—eyes like Tina's and their mom's according to the pictures Annie had seen—landed on Annie. "I was hoping to catch Annie."

Oh, no. Oh, no, no, no. Annie looked around, wanting to run, but then she wasn't able to make her feet move. Penny and Beth left in a flurry of movement and Jane just stood in that same spot.

Finally, Jane breathed out and pushed hair away from her face. "I don't know why I came here."

Annie didn't either, and she still didn't know what to say. "Congratulations."

Great. That staple. Not that it had worked out terribly with Peter.

"Thanks." Jane bit her lip, sat in the chair next to Annie and twisted to face her. Her hands were flat over her thighs and she blew bangs from her face. "Okay, I'm just going to come out and say it. I don't know how else to do it."

Annie stayed quiet. She was trying to think back over the last few days to see what had gotten hot enough under Jane's bottom to end their each-other-didn't-exist truce to come blame something on her.

Jane faced her. "I want to talk about that morning. When I found you and we talked."

Oh that. "Just let it be."

"I have. For years." She took a deep breath and then all once words started pouring out. "Peter and I were already dating. I came to tell you so you wouldn't be blindsided at school the next day. Then you said you were late and you stunned me and I forgot to tell you about Peter and I and then the next day you found out about us." Jane all but panted and slouched in her chair. "You two had broken up. Peter and I were always friends. I know it was a tight timeline in there from when y'all broke up and we got together, but it just happened. I wanted to tell you back then, but you wouldn't even look at me." Jane looked away from the table. "I mean, you unloaded that you thought you were pregnant and it was terrible and I felt horrible, but I honestly forgot why I had gone looking for you. The moment I left you, I remembered, but I didn't know what to say. A couple weeks went by and then I saw stuff in the trash and knew you'd gotten your period and that you were okay."

Annie just sat there. Wait…what now? She faced the table too and slouched all the same as Jane. "In all the years we still lived together after, why didn't you tell me?"

"You wouldn't stay in the same room with me long enough for me to say anything. Things weren't always great between us, so I left you be. After everything and some of the mean things I'd done, I was fine being the bad guy for you." Jane's breath was long and slow. "I didn't want to tell you now, because I didn't want you to think I was doing it to get cake out of you. I don't even care about the cake. I never have."

"I got the feeling that was Grandma more than anything."

Jane sat up. "Every time it came up, I told her no. I wanted you to know."

"Thank you." She looked to her sister. My God, she'd spent years being completely wrong about something because she'd chosen to disappear instead of face it. All the times she'd thrown Jane under the bus and thought terrible things and…she'd been wrong. Jane hadn't hooked up with Peter after their talk that morning. They were already together. Sure, the time was tight between Annie breaking up with Peter and Jane and Peter getting together, but they were already together before Annie had talked to her sister. Her chest ached at how wrong she'd been. If only she could have known this years ago. That moment in the bathroom could have put them on completely different paths. "It means a lot."

"You should probably thank Cade. I didn't want to say anything to you, but Peter nagged me constantly. Cade practically begged me last night, but I didn't know what to say or if you'd even believe me. And if you didn't believe me, it would make it worse. I just wanted to let sleeping dogs lie because I didn't want to hurt you more."

"Cade?"

Jane smiled. "Sorry. I probably wasn't supposed to say something. He got the principal to keep you occupied through all of halftime so he could talk to me."

But he'd said… "I see."

Jane caught her by the arm. "I refused last night. I was determined to let you keep your space. Peter was texting me after you got here and asking me again to please come talk to you."

That explained Cade's moodiness then after halftime. She couldn't believe he'd gone through that trouble for her.

They were quiet for a moment and Jane plucked a strip of celery off the table. She didn't eat it, but pulled it apart in strips. "He really likes you."

"I know."

"I don't think you know how much." Jane caught her gaze and went back to the celery. "He doesn't date a lot. Hardly ever really."

"He said there's not a girl he likes here."

Jane chuckled. "I can see him saying that. Anyway, to go from hardly dating at all to pleading me to talk with you, I think it says a lot about him."

Yes, it did. And she would always be grateful to him for that. "Do you think you could tell Tina to leave him alone?"

Jane winced. "I've tried."

"Cade thinks you're half of the instigator there."

"*Unknowing* instigator. Tina can be very…"

"Manipulative?"

Jane's smile was tight as she nodded. "Yeah. That's a good word for it."

"Cade's word for her, by the way, if you're wondering how much he doesn't like her."

"I was starting to get the feeling of how much he didn't like her." Jane tossed the last of the celery on the plate. "Tina is very… Well, she has a lot going on and a lot that she has planned out in her head. Things she's figured out aren't working for her."

"Cade was worried she was going to slit his tires. I told him to worry for my tires."

Jane chuckled. "Nah. She wouldn't do anything like that."

"I wouldn't put it past her. She blames me for everything." *And you do too.* Annie held that back. Then rethought it. Why exactly was she holding that back? If she ever wanted answers, this was probably her chance to get them. "Why did you—both—always blame me for what happened to your mom?"

Jane's gaze fell to her lap. She rubbed her arms. "I'm sorry for that. I really am. I knew the things I was saying were horrible, but I didn't realize how horrible. I think we both needed a whipping boy, and you were that boy."

Annie pulled her knees to her chest in the chair. She just needed something to hug. "I think of everything, you blaming me for your mom's death hurt the worst."

Jane nodded. "I know. And you should never forgive me for that. I could say I was young and didn't really know what was going on."

"You were young. We were the same age and I didn't know what was going on."

"But I knew what I was saying was mean."

Stupid tears were in Annie's eyes before she could even get what she wanted to say all the way out. "I think what hurt the worst is that you were like a sister to me for a little bit. When y'all first moved here, we played all the time. All I ever had was Grandma and Grandpa. They were great, but they weren't out with me in the yard digging up whatever we found and calling it treasure. Then it was like one day, everything changed."

Jane was blinking fast. She touched the corners of her eyes. "My period came. Tina was older and I went to her. She was, I don't know." She dabbed at wetness in her eyes. "I remember her being short with me and her saying over and over that mom was supposed to be there for that. And that mom wasn't there anymore, that she wouldn't be there for anything, and it was all your mom's fault." Jane sniffed. "She was upset that I didn't spend time with her and that I played with you a lot. It was just the two of us, she said."

Annie had the urge to reach out and touch her, so she did. She'd grown up having Grandma in that role. She'd never had her mom there to plan to look to for help. "I'm so sorry."

Fat tears were coming down Jane's cheeks now. "It's not your fault."

"But I'm still sorry your mom isn't here for you."

All at once, Jane turned and buried her face was against Annie's shoulder and neck. Annie froze as Jane pulled against her side, wadding her shirt up. Loud sobs came out of her. Jumbled words were all but shouted. "I didn't realize we were teaming up against you until later. Peter told me."

Right. Because Annie had more than likely vented to Peter. Penny appeared in the doorway behind Jane. Her eyes were wide and searching. Annie waved her off with a flick of her wrist and then patted Jane's back.

Jane sniffed really hard and sat up. Her eyes were red and puffed out. Tear stains marked her cheeks. "I'm so sorry. So very sorry. I know it wasn't your fault Mom died. I know it wasn't your mom's fault either. I hope you know that."

"I never believed either of us was at fault."

Jane wiped her eyes and tapped the back of her hand to the tip of her nose. She lightly chuckled. "Uh, I wasn't expecting all that."

"It's okay." Annie blinked off more of her own tears and found herself having to wipe her eyes too.

"If the only reason you never came home or aren't living here, or whatever, is because of me, I wanted to clear the air."

"I'm glad you did."

"I'm glad I did too." She breathed out and cleared her throat. "I'm sorry I didn't invite you to the wedding."

Annie laughed. "I know why you didn't. I wouldn't have wanted the invitation anyway."

Jane covered her hand and gave her squeeze. "But I would love it if you could be there."

Staying for the wedding would mean changing her flight though.

And unless she got someone to drive her to a bigger airport, that would mean she'd be in Turtle Pine for another week. And it would also mean missing another week for work, which would put the bakery in a serious bind because she had six birthday parties depending on her.

She bit her lip and suddenly hated that all her years of hard work and the responsibility it'd created coming down on top of her. "I'll see."

"No pressure. If you don't want to, I'll understand."

"It's not that. I would love to, but I'll miss my flight home and I have to be at work no later than Wednesday. I have six kids counting on me to make them birthday cakes they'll never forget."

"Oh." Jane nodded and her worried brows relaxed into a smile. "That makes sense. Don't get fired for staying, but maybe don't be such a stranger?"

Annie found herself smiling. "I won't be. I promise."

"The cakes you make are really pretty. I follow the bakery you work for on Facebook and they post all your cakes." Her brow dipped again. "At least, I hope they do."

"They do." And a part of her in the center of her chest softened all over. "Thank you."

Jane was worrying her lip this time as she stood. "And congratulations to you. Peter took me to see you graduate college. I was so proud and always wanted to tell you."

Oh dang, tears were back in her eyes. "I wish I had known you were there."

"I was afraid of upsetting you on your big day, but I yelled louder for you than anyone in our section was yelling. And I took a bunch of pictures."

"I'm glad to know you were there." Annie nodded and clearly

remembered the day she'd picked up her diploma. She'd been proud of herself and a lot of that had stemmed from the fact that she'd known she'd escaped Turtle Pine. Now here she was wanting back in. That was the honest truth. She did want back in. As much as she loved her job, she missed home.

Jane left a few moments later to take care of wedding stuff. In a haze Annie couldn't quite describe, she helped put away lunch things and was clearing the table when Cade came back. They said their goodbyes and left. Nobody asked her about Jane. She only gave a nod to Cade's questions and concerns that she was okay.

For once, when she nodded to that question, she really was okay. At least she thought she was. No, she was totally okay. Cade pulled into the lot by the bakery and gave her a puzzling look. "You sure you don't want me to take you home?"

"I'm sure. I want to make sure everything is put away like it's supposed to be."

"The rehearsal tonight will probably last a couple hours. I'll swing by and pick you up on my way home?"

"That would be great." She pressed a quick kiss on him and hopped out.

As the roar of his Jeep faded off in the distance, Annie walked around inside the bakery and tried to find her bearings. The bakery was her grounding place to keep her centered and to keep her head screwed on straight. If she couldn't figure things out here, it wasn't happening anywhere.

The building was so small compared to what she was used to in Houston, but as she looked at the walls that held so many memories, they made it seem three times the size. She'd lied before when she'd said she wanted to make sure everything was put away as it was supposed to be.

After delivering the cupcakes yesterday, she'd come back and cleaned up, put everything back in its place. She'd cleaned counters, shelves, even the refrigerators as she organized the leftover butter, eggs and milk.

All that was left was to walk around in the bakery and decide what she wanted. Maybe drink some coffee too. Coffee was definitely a good idea. No big decision should come on a half-asleep brain. She set the pot on, wandered into Grandpa's office and sat in the large chair that rocked back enough to make her feel like it was about to deposit her on the floor.

She kept a steady hand on the desk as she reclined. Grandma said she could take over here if she wanted. Of course, that could have been an offhand comment, but Annie had noticed the lack of her grandpa's presence in the bakery this week. Sure, his wrist was a factor there, but bumps and bruises and whatever had never stopped him from being in here when she was a kid. The man was in his late seventies. He was probably ready to retire. Not that he needed her to take over the bakery so he could.

Turtle Pine might wish for that though. Or wish for someone to come in and buy him out. She flicked at the papers on his desk and caught sight of a stack of drawings. She flipped through them and studied what was maybe birthday cakes. Grandpa could create what he wanted out of icing, but drawing with a pencil wasn't his specialty.

She turned the images around as she looked at them. It'd been a while since she'd seen his drawings, but after a few minutes, she recalled the way he marked lines for this and that. She turned to another and found the marks for Jane's cake with an invitation stapled to the top. Probably a note for the wedding colors. Looked like he'd been planning four tiers of something. It wasn't finished.

Pillars supported the sections high in the air. Marks weren't even made yet for what sort of frosting design. Annie grabbed a pencil and went to mark on the drawing. Before the tip met the paper, she stopped and found a new sheet.

She took off the pillars and made the sections of cake thicker to get the same height without the spaces between. Jane had always had a thing for fairies. They were actually still all over the second floor of Grandma's house. By the ones on the invitation, that was carrying over into her wedding. Annie decorated with twirling green vines instead of a thick row of any sort of design. It would be a smooth cake decorated like a garden. She added flowers up the side and drew an explosion of flowers and leaves off the top where the bride and groom figurines would stand.

She leaned back from her drawing, turning the page for a better angle. It wasn't quite right. It was probably going to be too much cake, if there ever was such a thing, but she added miniature sections of four tiers around the center anyway. Each mini-cake was decorated the same as the other. She added fairies over all the smaller ones and turned them to look at the bride and groom atop the main section.

There. Now she was getting something, but still it needed more. A fairy wedding was nothing without a real blanket of flowers. She added quick sketches of flowers and greenery all around the cakes so that the cakes appeared to grow as white tree stumps in a garden. She studied the picture she'd drawn as her fingers itched to get busy.

This was a cake to decorate in a week. Or at least a few days with a lot of help. Jane's wedding was in—she squinted at the clock—twenty-one or so hours. But the reception wasn't for at least twenty-two hours. She looked back to her drawing. It was going to be cutting it close.

It would also mean she'd miss her flight home. She pushed hair away from her face. Okay, so she'd need to get a ride to a bigger airport by Tuesday. Her grandma wanted this the most, so she could take her. Or Annie would just have to borrow their car and get herself to the airport.

She counted up rows of cake. There were a lot. She wasn't sure if she was crazy-girl laughing or seriously sobbing. This was seventy-eight rounds of varying diameters. Over half were smallish sizes that she could get out of a few batches of cake. A good number of them were going to take a lot of cake. She rubbed her chin, trying to figure out who was dependable to help bake. The only answer she got was her grandpa, and he was out with his wrist.

If she had a dishwasher though, that would help. Anyone she knew to possibly call was going to be at the rehearsal dinner for the next couple of hours. Paula was an option, but if the woman wasn't working herself, Annie feared she'd be a distraction. Annie pushed out of her chair, filled up her coffee mug and got busy on the main section. She dug out the rounds, set the oven temps and got busy measuring, weighing and sorting ingredients.

She kicked up the radio and slid the first of many batches into the oven. She baked and turned out sections across the front tables and anywhere she could get them, kind of like when she'd turned out the cupcakes. She had another batch going in as Cade's Jeep pulled back up outside. A little sadness filled her because now that she'd started this, she wouldn't be spending tonight with him.

Then again, because of this, she could be here for a few more days. Definitely worth giving up tonight for. She just had to survive the next twenty-four hours. She set another pot of coffee on as the back door opened and he paused in the doorway. "Wow."

She turned. "How'd the rehearsal go?"

"As planned." He walked in slowly and looked around. "What are you doing?"

"Jane's cake."

He frowned. "Did she ask you to do that today?"

She shook her head. There was enough coffee in the pot to get one more mug out of it. She fixed it up and set on a new pot. "No. I want to. Can you do me a favor?"

"Sure."

She liked that he didn't hesitate. "Go to the grocery store and buy all the flowers they have—except roses. I don't need those."

"Flowers. No roses."

"Right."

A brow lifted. "All of them?"

"Every available one."

"Anything else?"

She set her coffee to cool and started on the dishes to push out the next batch to fill the ovens while they baked the current ones. "Um, maybe something for me to eat later for supper? And then something for later tonight. And breakfast in the morning."

He studied her. "You're planning to work all night."

"I don't have a choice if I want to finish."

He grinned. "All right. Do I have time to swing by my house?"

"Oh yeah. I won't need the flowers until tomorrow. I just don't want to forget them."

"Great. I'll be back."

She got back to making her next set. Then the next and the next. Cade popped back in about an hour later carrying bag after bag after bag of flowers. She directed him to put them in the refrigerator as she had her hands busy with measuring. He made several trips with the flowers and then more with groceries. She didn't care what kind of food. She'd be fine eating jerky and raisins.

He'd also changed clothes from his khakis and nice shirt to running pants and tennis shoes. He came back through to wash his hands, only he didn't stop there. He filled up the sink. "I'll wash and you bake again?"

She blushed. "I wasn't going to ask you to do that."

"Happy to. I don't know what made you change your mind, but I want to be here to help."

"Thank you."

Hours ticked over as she made cake after cake after cake. As yet another batch of cake went in, she stopped for a quick stretch and another cup of coffee. The coffee was wearing thin and the hours were getting late. Cade was yawning in the corner and she couldn't start that or she'd never make it.

"You can go whenever you want. You were a huge help."

He stretched his arms overhead. "I'm not leaving you here."

Oh, there went some more of her heart, getting all warm and cozy. "I don't have to take pictures tomorrow. I don't want your eyes to be dark and baggy for the camera."

"I'll be fine."

"Cade."

"Annie," he countered and stood with his hands over his chest. "I'm not leaving you."

She sighed. "At least sit down and take a break. Grandpa's chair in his office is really comfortable."

"I will after a while. I promise."

She got started on frosting with a few batches of pink, yellow, blue, purple and nearly every other color she could think up. And then green. Several more bags of green. Cade came up behind her and rubbed her shoulders. "You need a break."

"I can't. If I stop, I'll never get going again."

"Twenty minutes. Stop for twenty minutes."

"I can sleep after it's all done. I'm about to start assembling and frosting. It'll be something new and I'll perk back up, I promise."

He didn't nag her further and she collected the base pieces of the big center and layered frosting between and set a rod in them to hold them. Then came the next layer, then the next and the next after that until the final one. She trimmed the edges to match and frosted all the way around.

She bit her lip. The top was too high to detail. She needed a stool that wasn't wobbly to reach up there. Or a shorter table. One shorter like the one that the cake would be served from. It would be easier to deliver the cake if she did the rest of the assembly on-site. She stepped back and checked the clock. Five a.m.

"What is it?" Cade appeared from her Grandpa's office. She wasn't sure he looked any fresher than when he'd left the room, but a couple hours of sleep had to be better for him than nothing.

"What time does someone get to the church?"

"Probably about eight or so. Service begins at nine."

She winced. "It would be easier and faster to assemble there, but I would need in the reception hall."

He wrapped her in a hug from behind and kissed the top of her head. "I can probably help you out there. Mrs. Billie has a key and she runs every morning. I bet I can catch her."

Oh, sweet heavens. "That would be perfect."

"One condition."

She was almost afraid to ask, but she didn't have much of a choice. "I'll do it."

"Sit down and get some rest while I'm gone."

That was…okay. But only because she was at a standstill if she planned to finish at the church. Cade walked her to the office and gave her a kiss. She reclined and found her eyes closing. Next thing she knew, he was shaking her by the shoulder. She started and sat forward. "You're already back?"

He was grinning. "You've been out for about an hour."

She leapt out of her chair. "Oh my goodness."

"I've already loaded all the cake and flowers. Tell me what to grab."

Bless him. She'd needed that hour of rest and grabbed up her frosting, rods, platters and bag of decorating utensils. Half the hard battle was over with.

Chapter Sixteen

Annie tucked another fairy in place, fluffed the greenery and flowers around the cake and ran to the back as wedding music sounded out again, announcing the end of the ceremony. She had frosting on her in places she didn't want it and her clothes were a huge mess.

When she'd gone after fairy figurines from Jane's collection at Grandma's, she'd had the forethought to grab the pink dress she'd flown to Turtle Pine in. With moments to spare, she did a quick change of clothes into something presentable. From the neck down. From the neck up, all bets were off. Her hair was still in the bun or whatever halfway put-up thing she'd finagled last night when she'd started this epic, ridiculous journey. Best she could hope for was that there wasn't any frosting smeared on her cheek.

Annie stood back in the hallway leading to the kitchen as the front door opened and a photographer walked in the room backwards. Jane came in wearing an off-the-shoulder beautiful white gown. It was fitted across her chest, down to her waist. From there, the lightest-looking silk flowed around her. She appeared to be floating. She was laughing and smiling and part of Annie's heart she didn't know was alive filled with warmth and stretched at the seams.

Annie waited in her spot as the newlyweds got halfway through the room and Jane stopped. She covered her mouth. Peter's gaze froze on the cake and the photographer snapped it all up. Before the room crowded in, Annie stepped from the hallway.

Even though the cake was right up her sister's alley, Jane hadn't approved it, vetted it or anything. Annie fidgeting with her fingers as she weaved her way between tables. "Congratulations, you two."

Jane's gaze swung to hers and she came at Annie with her arms out, tears dripping over her cheek. "Oh, Annie. It's beautiful."

She met her sister's hug and gave her an equally hard squeeze. "I hoped you would like it."

"I love it." Jane leaned back but didn't let go of Annie's hands.

Annie led the two of them to the cake. "I put your other cake back, but we can get it out if you want."

Jane's fingers were over her mouth. She went to touch something but pulled her hand back. "Oh my God. You went and got those from Grandma's."

"You can touch them." Dang. Those tears were contagious.

Jane cleared her throat. She still hadn't let go of Annie's hand. "It's gorgeous. Thank you. How long have you been doing this?"

"Since last night."

Jane and Peter both blinked at her.

She lifted a shoulder and that's when the rest of the wedding party started their way in. Cade was by her side in a moment and grinned. He kissed her forehead. "Did you get it done in time?"

She laughed and wrapped an arm around his back. "I think I was changing clothes as they were walking out."

"Annie!" A little flower girl fairy came running across the reception hall. Big, sparkling wings flapped behind her and flowers were all in her hair.

Annie caught Katie up to her side. "Well, aren't you a pretty flower fairy."

The girl grinned and studied Annie. She pulled a flower out of her hair and stuck it in Annie's. "Now you're pretty too."

They all laughed and Annie lowered the wiggling girl as she set her eyes on the cake. Annie shook her head. "I think I need more than a flower for this hair."

Jane's smile was still as big as she'd ever seen it. "My makeup and stuff for my hair is in the back where we used to have Sunday school, if you want to use it."

"Thanks." She laughed. "I'll head that way."

She didn't make it far before her grandma was at her side. She caught Annie's face in her cold hands. "Look what you did. I always knew you could do it."

Grandpa came up and looked the table over and gave her a nod. "I'm impressed." He held up his hands. "Does that mean I can finally take this stupid thing off?"

Grandma's eyes widened and then she laughed with a toss of her head. "Go ahead."

He took the wrist brace off and they all stared at him with their mouths wide open. "Don't blame me. This was all your grandma's idea to get Annie home."

Annie couldn't help it. She laughed. She turned around and spotted someone so familiar standing there. Familiar but also a stranger. She eyed her. "Mary?"

The young, shy girl she barely remembered waved. "Hi, Annie."

"Look how pretty you are."

Her younger sister was gorgeous with her red, curly hair and wearing a light green bridesmaid dress. "Thanks."

"Where's Dad?"

Jane rolled her eyes. "He couldn't get off work."

That was no big surprise. She turned and was met with two faces of young boys. Jane had a hand on either of their shoulders. "Annie, meet your nephews. Pat and James."

The boys shook her hand, but they were eyeing cake. Not just her cake, but the groom's cake too. And the buffet table. They definitely had their mom's tendency to set their sights on something they wanted. Speaking of their mom. She took a deep breath. If she was going to stay in Turtle Pine, this was going to be part of it. "Where's Tina at?"

Pat, the oldest one, shrugged. "I don't know. Said she didn't feel well and left."

Jane frowned and passed a look to Annie. "It's not you. She was disappointed when I told her Dad called this morning and said he couldn't be here."

Tina being the oldest meant she was the only one of the three of them who'd ever really known their dad. She ran that thought over in her mind and found herself pitying Tina. Tina had been old enough to understand exactly what was going on back then, and to make matters worse, her dad all but abandoned her. Annie nodded, understanding Tina more than she'd ever considered before. "Let me get cleaned up." She glanced around at all the doorways. "If I can find where to go in this maze."

Cade chuckled and placed his hand at her back. "I'll show you."

He led her through the twists and turns of the church. The farther they got away from the reception and the laughter of the people from inside, the closer they got to sanctuary. He stopped at a door and opened it for her.

Cade walked in and sat on a chair. He tapped his fingertips together. "I noticed you missed your flight home."

She smiled and sat next to him. "I did."

"That means you're here for another week."

She sighed. "No. I have to find a way to a bigger airport. I have to be home and back at work by Wednesday."

He studied her with a frown getting stronger on his brow. "You have to? Or are you choosing to?"

"Have to," she confirmed. "I have six little kids depending on me to make their birthday cakes. I can't push that much work off on my coworkers. They'll have to cancel orders."

"And then?"

"And then…" She breathed. "I don't know. I have other things I'm scheduled to bake, but this far in advance, the bakery can hopefully start making arrangements for some of it. I may have to stick around for a couple weeks longer than I'm thinking. I don't remember what's on my schedule."

He sat back and looked at her. "Are you saying what I think you're saying?"

"I would really like it if you could fly home with me this week and help me pack. If you can get off. Or next week, if you need to give more notice at work."

He nodded. "I can get off. I don't know if I can stay until you come back, but I can go out there initially."

"That would be great."

He chuckle slipped out of him. "I really didn't think you would come back."

She sat up and searched him. "You don't want me here?"

He grinned and cupped her cheek. "I want you here. I just didn't think I could get you to stay."

She leaned forward so her head rested on his. "You can't get me to leave."

"I love you."

"I love you."

"I'm going to marry you sometime soon."

Everything about all of this settled comfortably in her bones and felt so right. "I'm counting on it."

"But I'm not going to ask you today."

She searched his eyes, not caring when he planned to ask. "I'll be ready to say yes when you do."

"Good. Practice that for tomorrow. Because today is your sister's day, and I want you to have your own day all to yourself."

"I like that plan." She kissed him and ended up across his lap with her arms around his neck. "Do you think anyone would notice if we stayed in here?"

Giggles from a certain little girl started down the hall. Then the door opened and the little flower fairy stood in the doorway. "Hurry up! Aunt Jane says we can't have cake without you there to cut it."

"I'm coming." She kissed Cade again before pushing out of his lap. "Getting interrupted by her feels like practice."

"I know something else we can practice a little later on."

She tossed him a wink. "I'm counting down the minutes until we can."

About the Author

Keri Ford brings sexy contemporary romance to the American South. With a sprinkling of men in suits and women in high heels, you'll most likely find four-wheeler riding, ball cap wearing fellas trying to sweet-talk sundress wearing ladies in Keri's books. Raised in the country in South Arkansas, Keri shares this flavor of life in her books. Glass of sweet tea at your elbow while you read is not required, but strongly recommended. To learn more about Keri, visit www.keriford.com.

A little hard wood and a little spice is enough to get this fire smoking.

Naked Desire
© 2014 Desiree Holt

Naked Cowboys, Book 5

After a shattering divorce, Cynthia Dellinger is left with almost nothing except her most precious possession—her grandfather's secret barbecue spice rub recipe, which made her ex a fortune.

In Saddler's Wells, she hopes to build a business—and maybe a new life—on the strength of that recipe. But she's totally unprepared for her sizzling attraction to the artisan carpenter her new friends send her way.

Jesse Orosco is ready to roll up his sleeves to renovate Cyn's storefront, but it's the self-doubt lurking in her beautiful eyes he wants to tackle first. The five-foot-nothing red-headed dynamo makes his mouth water, and not just because of the tantalizing aromas drifting from the back of her shop.

The buzz about the rub's mysterious ingredient has customers lining up for more, and soon everyone who tries it is making beautiful music in the bedroom—including Cyn and Jesse. But her reluctance to go public with their relationship—and someone in town with a jealous bone to pick—could drive a wedge between Cyn and her smoking-hot cowboy.

Warning: Contains a sexy carpenter with calluses in all the right places, a vulnerable woman who's locked away more than a secret ingredient in her wounded heart, and a town full of matchmakers with an appetite for love.

Enjoy the following excerpt for Naked Desire:

"You're going to need help turning that place you rented into a store, and we've got just the person to help you." She raised her voice. "Hey, Jesse. Come on over here. I've got someone I want you to meet."

Cyn looked to where her friend was pointing and saw what could only be described as a luscious mouthful of a man heading toward the door. A shade under six feet, the T-shirt and faded jeans he wore molded to a lean, muscular body. When he turned toward them, he moved with such a fluid grace Cyn's pulse thumped in response.

"Wait, wait, wait," she protested.

She had no idea who this was, but she was hardly ready to discuss business—or anything else—with a man who looked like this. How many years had it been since her body responded to the sight of a man this way? And why now, when she was so desperately trying to pick up the torn threads of her life? When she felt so vulnerable? What was wrong with her anyway?

Amy raised her eyebrows? "Wait? For what?"

"B-But I've barely signed the lease on the store," she stuttered. "I have to think about what the inside should look like. I mean—"

"Cyn." Georgie laughed. "Take a breath. This is the first day of the rest of your life. And look what you've got. A new business and a gorgeous man to help you do the build out. I can certainly tell you doing that turned out well for me."

"Really well," Amy teased.

Cyn was still trying to get her brain on track when the man arrived at their table, flashing even white teeth in a wide grin. Her brain kept trying to tell her she was a forty-two-year-old has-been but her body was saying *yum*.

Ohmigod!

"Nice to see you, ladies." He bestowed a brief kiss on the cheek of everyone he knew. Then his eyes landed on Cyn. "I see you're adding to the scenery around here." He held out his hand. "Jesse Orosco."

"C-Cyn Dellinger." She held out her hand. "Nice to meet you."

Eyes black as onyx blazed from beneath lashes any woman would kill for, and when he smiled, a dimple winked from one corner of his mouth. The touch of his warm hand sent electricity sizzling through her arm to various parts of her body. Cyn swallowed a gasp. Shockingly, between his looks and his touch, the man she was staring at stirred things in her she had been sure were dead and buried. Or maybe had never even stirred to life.

Down, Cyn. You're here for business, not sex. If you even remember what that is. Besides, he's way younger than you are. Maybe nine or ten years. Good. That age difference makes a good barrier. I hope.

"Nice meeting you too." He flashed a devastating white smile.

"Jesse is the most talented craftsman around." Amy grinned at the hunk. "He did a lot of work at our ranch when Buck first bought it."

"For me too," Georgie chimed in. "He did all the finish work that Cade didn't have the experience for. When you get back there today, remind me to show it to you."

Jesse glanced from one to the other, one eyebrow cocked, a quizzical look on his face. "Thanks for the endorsement, ladies, but what's this all about?"

"Cyn's new to Saddle Wells," Reenie said. "She moved here recently and rented that last empty space on Main Street. She's got a specialty item she'll be selling and she needs someone to help her turn the space into an attractive store."

"And we think you're the right one to take on the job," Amy added.

Cyn felt as if she'd somehow lost control of the situation and it was running away from her.

"Hold on a sec," she interrupted. "Please." She let out a breath. "Ladies. Take a minute. He probably has plenty of work on his plate already." She looked up at him. "Right? I don't want you to feel like they're pushing you in to something."

His laugh was a devastating sexual weapon all by itself.

"Not to worry. I've known most of them a long time. Anyway, you're actually in luck. I finished a big job last week and was taking a little breather."

"Hmm. Well, I don't want to intrude on your down time."

"Not a problem." He dragged an empty chair over from a nearby table, turned it around and straddled it, resting his forearms on the back. "So tell me about this store."

Cyn tried to organize her thoughts but her brain seemed to have stopped functioning. Heat crept up her cheeks and she cursed herself for the uncontrollable blush. At forty-two, she found herself suddenly tongue-tied and self-conscious. You'd think she'd never talked to a good-looking man before. Well, not one like this. Frank had been handsome but in a different way. And as the marriage had crumbled, he'd become less and less appealing.

Get it together, kiddo. This is the next step in the liberation of Cyn Dellinger.

He plans to take the wander right out of her wanderlust.

Texas Bossa Nova
© 2015 Cynthia D'Alba

Texas Montgomery Mavericks, Book 5

Magda Hobbs's job as ranch housekeeper—and its daily dose of cowboys—wreaked havoc on her libido. Especially one certain cowboy she couldn't resist. Scared of going down the same path as her mother, Magda jumped on her motorcycle and hit the road.

Five months later, her father's mild heart attack has forced her back to Whispering Springs. While she's grateful for the cleaning job at one of the Montgomery ranch houses, she's not so thrilled one of the cowboys she's looking after is the one she fell for last spring.

Reno Montgomery's parents hiring a housekeeper for him and his brother is a nice surprise, but he's shocked to discover it's Magda, the woman who up and left just when things were getting serious between them.

When a freak snowstorm cuts off the outside world, the isolation rekindles their desire. But when the weather and the roads clear, Reno has to work hard and fast to keep the woman of his dreams from accelerating right out of his life again.

Warning: Contains a woman born with a bad case of wanderlust, and a cowboy determined to show her that life's a dance that doesn't have to two-step her out of his life.

Enjoy the following excerpt for Texas Bossa Nova:

By six the next morning, Reno and Darren were out of the house and in the field repairing a fence that'd taken on a huge tree limb during the ice storm last week and lost. There'd been no cattle in the pasture, so they'd been in no hurry to fix it. However, Reno had pushed Darren into getting on it today, mostly so Reno didn't have to face Magda just yet.

They'd left a note on the front door for Magda and the door unlocked. No one in their right mind would come all the way to their house to rob it. It was too far out and there was absolutely nothing of value in there.

About ten o'clock, as he was pulling the wire tight on the fence, a Harley-Davidson Fat Boy motorcycle roared past them and up their drive.

"Think that's her?" Darren asked.

"Yep. That's her bike."

"Sweet. I'd love to take her for a ride."

Reno glared at him.

"I mean the bike, not the lady," Darren clarified. "Man, you're touchy."

While Reno privately agreed with his brother, no way was he saying that aloud. "Ah, well, I hear she's pretty particular about who she lets ride her Fat Boy."

"So many jokes I could make, but seeing as you've got a stick up your butt about our new housekeeper, I'll keep my mouth shut."

"Probably for the best."

At about noon, Reno's cell phone trilled and he pulled it out of his pocket. "Hello?"

"Reno? This is Magda. Magda Hobbs."

The sound of her voice made his heart leap, pushing all the air from his lungs. As though there could be more than one Magda. As if he didn't hear her voice every night in his dreams.

He drew in some air to calm his racing heart. It didn't work. "Hi. I guess you got in the house without a problem." Man, he hated how breathless and excited he sounded. He was a much better poker player than this.

"I did. I wondered if you guys were coming back to the house for lunch today."

Reno looked at Darren. "You want to head back for lunch?"

Darren nodded.

"Yeah, that'd be great." He wondered how he would ever swallow around the boulder that had lodged in his throat the minute he'd heard her say his name.

"Okay," she said with a slight hesitation in her voice. "I'll see what I can find, but your cabinets are a little bare."

Reno forced a chuckle, a little embarrassed that she'd found their cabinets basically empty. "Noticed that, did you? Honestly, we just haven't had time to get to the store. You may have noticed on your way over that we kind of live in the middle of nowhere."

"I noticed. I'll have lunch ready in about thirty minutes."

Reno slipped his phone back in his pocket. "Thirty minutes." Great. That gave him a whole half an hour to get himself together.

Thirty minutes later, Reno parked the work truck at the back door and Darren hopped out. From the truck, Reno watched as Darren opened the door, took one step inside and stopped. He backed out, toed off his boots and reentered.

Not wanting to make the same mistake, Reno left his boots on the back porch and walked in. He was greeted by the aroma of grilled ham and...he sniffed again...toast?

"Hello, Reno," Magda said. "I have grilled cheese and ham

sandwiches and tomato soup. Best I could do with what you guys had in the cabinets."

"Sounds wonderful. Thanks."

"Water? Coke? Tea?" Magda asked.

"I'll get it," he replied, heading for the refrigerator to grab a cold water.

Darren was already at the table, his sandwich half-gone. He took another bite and moaned. "So good."

Reno sat and Magda set a bowl of soup and a sandwich in front of him. "Thanks."

She joined the guys at the table. "I want us to get off to the right start," she said, leaning forward and placing her arms on the table. "I wouldn't have sought out this job. We are all really too close in age for me to feel one-hundred percent comfortable in the situation. However, I needed a job and your parents made me a very generous offer that I'd have been a fool to turn down. But…" She paused and waited until she could meet both their gazes before she continued. "But I want this to work out, which means there will be no kissing or touching or trapping me in the corner. No inappropriate comments. No sexual suggestions. I cook, clean and do laundry for you, but that's it. I'm not here to share a bed or catch a husband. Have I made myself clear?"

Reno swallowed the bite of sandwich he'd been chewing. "Clear. And I completely agree. Darren?" He looked over at his brother.

"Got it. Damn, Magda, you're one straight-shooting talker."

She leaned back in the chair. "Yep, I am. Another thing is that I expect you two not to make my job even more difficult by being total slobs. That means leave your mud, manure and blood-coated boots outside. If I find them in the house, you'll find them outside in a tree where they'll land when I toss them out the door. Understood?"

Both men nodded, and Reno suppressed a smile. Darren had no idea that Magda was serious, nor how their lives were going to change.

That evening, Magda had dinner ready when they got home. She also had a list of supplies and food stock that she needed to get for the house. As at lunch, Magda joined them at the kitchen table to talk about her list and how they wanted to cover expenses. Reno noticed that while she would sit with them at the table, she'd yet to eat with them.

"Aren't you going to eat?" Reno asked around a bite of roast.

"I've eaten," Magda said. "Thank you. Now about this list…"

Reno pulled his wallet from his back pocket, pulled out a credit card and pushed it across the table toward her. "Charge them."

She eyed the card as though he were handing her a lit stick of dynamite. "Um, don't you think the merchants might figure out that I'm not Reno Montgomery?"

Darren chuckled. "Damn straight. He's ugly as a rock. You, on the other hand, are as beautiful as—"

He didn't get to finish his statement. Magda slapped the back of his head.

"Ouch. What'd you do that for?" Darren rubbed his head.

"I told you today. No inappropriate comments."

Reno jerked his glass of iced tea to his mouth to keep from laughing.

"That wasn't inappropriate. I was just going to say—" He ducked his head to the side as Magda lifted her hand. "Never mind. I wasn't going to say anything."

She smiled and placed her hand in her lap.

It's all about the story...

Romance

HORROR

Retro ROMANCE

www.samhainpublishing.com

3 3264 03426 0474

CPSIA information can be obtained at www.ICGtesting.com
Printed in the USA
LVOW10s2136041115
461187LV00003B/136/P